PEN

THE BEST

Paul Gallico was born in New York City, of Italian and Austrian parentage, in 1897, and attended Columbia University. From 1922 to 1936 he worked on the *New York Daily News* as sports editor, columnist and assistant managing editor. In 1936 he bought a house on top of a hill at Salcombe in South Devon and settled down with a Great Dane and twenty-three assorted cats. It was in 1941 that he made his name with *The Snow Goose*, a classic story of Dunkirk which became a world-wide best-seller. Having served as a gunner's mate in the U.S. Navy in 1918, he was again active as a war correspondent with the American Expeditionary Force in 1944. Paul Gallico, who later lived in Monaco, was a first-class fencer and a keen sea-fisherman. He wrote over 40 books which include *Jennie* (1950), *The Small Miracle* (1952), *Snowflake* (1952), *Love of Seven Dolls* (1954), *Ludmila* (1955), *Thomasina* (1957), *Too Many Ghosts* (1961), *Scruffy* (1962), *Love, Let Me Not Hunger* (1963), *Flowers for Mrs Harris* (1963), *The Hand of Mary Constable* (1964), *The Steadfast Man*, a scholarly study of St Patrick, *The Hurricane Story* (1959), a 'biography' of the famous fighter, *Mrs Harris, M.P.* (1965), *The Day Jean-Pierre Went Round the World* (1965), *The Man Who was Magic* (1966), *The Story of Silent Night* (1967), *Manxmouse* (1968), *The Poseidon Adventure* (1969), *The Matilda* (1970), *Zoo Gang* (1971), *Honourable Cat* (1972), *The Boy Who Invented the Bubble Gun* (1974), *Mrs Harris Goes to Moscow* (1974) and *Miracle in the Wilderness* (1975). A posthumous work, *Beyond the Poseidon Adventure*, was published in 1978. Paul Gallico, one of the most prolific and professional of American authors, died in July 1976. He was married four

THE BEST OF
PAUL GALLICO

THE SNOW GOOSE

THE SMALL MIRACLE

LOVE OF SEVEN DOLLS

LUDMILA

PAUL GALLICO

PENGUIN BOOKS

PENGUIN BOOKS

Published by the Penguin Group
27 Wrights Lane, London w8 5tz, England
Viking Penguin Inc., 40 West 23rd Street, New York, New York 10010, USA
Penguin Books Australia Ltd, Ringwood, Victoria, Australia
Penguin Books Canada Ltd, 2801 John Street, Markham, Ontario, Canada l3r 1b4
Penguin Books (NZ) Ltd, 182–190 Wairau Road, Auckland 10, New Zealand

Penguin Books Ltd, Registered Offices: Harmondsworth, Middlesex, England

The Snow Goose first published in Great Britain by Michael Joseph in
November 1941. Copyright © 1941 by the Estate of the late Paul Gallico.
The Small Miracle first published in Great Britain by Michael Joseph in
November 1951. Copyright © 1951 by the Estate of the late Paul Gallico.
Love of Seven Dolls first published in Great Britain by Michael Joseph in
September 1954. Copyright © 1954 by the Estate of the late Paul Gallico.
Ludmila first published in Great Britain by Michael Joseph in 1955.
Copyright © 1955 by the Estate of the late Paul Gallico.

This omnibus first published by Michael Joseph 1988
Published in Penguin Books 1990
1 3 5 7 9 10 8 6 4 2

Copyright © the Estate of the late Paul Gallico, 1988
All rights reserved

Made and printed in Great Britain by
Richard Clay Ltd, Bungay, Suffolk

Contents

THE SNOW GOOSE   1

THE SMALL MIRACLE   33

LOVE OF SEVEN DOLLS   59

LUDMILA   171

THE SNOW GOOSE

THE GREAT MARSH lies on the Essex coast between the village of Chelmbury and the ancient Saxon oyster-fishing hamlet of Wickaeldroth. It is one of the last of the wild places of England, a low, far-reaching expanse of grass and reeds and half-submerged meadowlands ending in the great saltings and mud flats and tidal pools near the restless sea.

Tidal creeks and estuaries and the crooked, meandering arms of many little rivers whose mouths lap at the edge of the ocean cut through the sodden land that seems to rise and fall and breathe with the recurrence of the daily tides. It is desolate, utterly lonely, and made lonelier by the calls and cries of the wildfowl that make their homes in the marshlands and saltings – the wild geese and the gulls, the teal and widgeon, the redshanks and curlews that pick their way through the tidal pools. Of human habitants there are none, and none are seen, with the occasional exception of a wild-fowler or native oyster-fishermen, who still ply a trade already ancient when the Normans came to Hastings.

[3]

Greys and blues and soft greens are the colours, for when the skies are dark in the long winters, the many waters of the beaches and marshes reflect the cold and sombre colour. But sometimes, with sunrise and sunset, sky and land are aflame with red and golden fire.

Hard by one of the winding arms of the little River Aelder runs the embankment of an old sea wall, smooth and solid, without a break, a bulwark to the land against the encroaching sea. Deep into a salting some three miles from the English Channel it runs, and there turns north. At the corner its face is gouged, broken, and shattered. It has been breached, and at the breach the hungry sea has already entered and taken for its own the land, the wall, and all that stood there.

At low water the blackened and ruptured stones of the ruins of an abandoned lighthouse show above the surface, with here and there, like buoy markers, the top of a sagging fence-post. Once this lighthouse abutted on the sea and was a beacon on the Essex coast. Time shifted land and water, and its usefulness came to an end.

Lately it served again as a human habitation. In it there lived a lonely man. His body was warped, but his heart was filled with love for wild and hunted things. He was ugly to look upon, but he created great beauty. It is about him, and a child who came to know him and see beyond the grotesque form that housed him to what lay within, that this story is told.

[4]

It is not a story that falls easily and smoothly into sequence. It has been garnered from many sources and from many people. Some of it comes in the form of fragments from men who looked upon strange and violent scenes. For the sea has claimed its own and spreads its rippled blanket over the site, and the great white bird with the black-tipped pinions that saw it all from the beginning to the end has returned to the dark, frozen silences of the northlands whence it came.

In the late spring of 1930 Philip Rhayader came to the abandoned lighthouse at the mouth of the Aelder. He bought the light and many acres of marshland and salting surrounding it.

He lived and worked there alone the year round. He was a painter of birds and of nature, who, for reasons, had withdrawn from all human society. Some of the reasons were apparent on his fortnightly visits to the little village of Chelmbury for supplies, where the natives looked askance at his misshapen body and dark visage. For he was a hunchback and his left arm was crippled, thin and bent at the wrist, like the claw of a bird.

They soon became used to his queer figure, small but powerful, the massive, dark, bearded head set just slightly below the mysterious mound on his back, the glowing eyes and the clawed hand, and marked him off as 'that queer painter chap that lives down to light-house'.

Physical deformity often breeds hatred of humanity in men. Rhayader did not hate; he loved very greatly, man, the animal kingdom, and all nature. His heart was filled with pity and understanding. He had mastered his handicap, but he could not master the rebuffs he suffered, due to his appearance. The thing that drove him into seclusion was his failure to find anywhere a return of the warmth that flowed from him. He repelled women. Men would have warmed to him had they got to know him. But the mere fact that an effort was being made hurt Rhayader and drove him to avoid the person making it.

He was twenty-seven when he came to the Great Marsh. He had travelled much and fought valiantly before he made the decision to withdraw from a world in which he could not take part as other men. For all the artist's sensitivity and woman's tenderness locked in his barrel breast, he was very much a man.

In his retreat he had his birds, his painting, and his boat. He owned a sixteen-footer, which he sailed with wonderful skill. Alone, with no eyes to watch him, he managed well with his deformed hand, and he often used his strong teeth to handle the sheets of his billowing sails in a tricky blow.

He would sail the tidal creeks and estuaries and out to sea, and would be gone for days at a time, looking for new species of birds to photograph or sketch, and he became an adept at netting them to add to his collection of tamed wildfowl in the pen near his studio that formed the nucleus of a sanctuary.

He never shot over a bird, and wild-fowlers were not welcome near his premises. He was a friend to all things wild, and the wild things repaid him with their friendship.

Tamed in his enclosures were the geese that came winging down the coast from Iceland and Spitzbergen each October, in great skeins that darkened the sky and filled the air with the rushing noise of their passage — the brown-bodied pink-feet, white-breasted barnacles, with their dark necks and clowns' masks, the wild white fronts with black-barred breasts, and many species of wild ducks — widgeon, mallard, pintails, teal, and shovellers.

Some were pinioned, so that they would remain there as a sign and signal to the wild ones that came down at each winter's beginning that here were food and sanctuary.

Many hundreds came and remained with him all through the cold weather from October to the early spring, when they migrated north again to their breeding-grounds below the ice rim.

Rhayader was content in the knowledge that when storms blew, or it was bitter cold and food was scarce, or the big punt guns of the distant bag hunters roared, his birds were safe; that he had gathered to the sanctuary and security of his own arms and heart these many wild and beautiful creatures who knew and trusted him.

They would answer the call of the north in the spring, but in the fall they would come back, barking and whooping and honking in the autumn sky, to circle the landmark of the old light and drop to earth nearby to be his guests again — birds that he well remembered and recognised from the previous year.

And this made Rhayader happy, because he knew that implanted somewhere in their beings was the germ knowledge of his existence and his safe haven, that this knowledge had become a part of them and, with the coming of the grey skies and the winds from the north, would send them unerringly back to him.

For the rest, his heart and soul went into the painting of the country in which he lived and its creatures. There are not many Rhayaders extant. He hoarded them jealously, piling them up in his lighthouse and the store-rooms above by the hundreds. He was not satisfied with them, because as an artist he was uncompromising.

But the few that have reached the market are masterpieces, filled with the glow and colours of marsh-reflected light, the feel of flight, the push of birds breasting a morning wind bending the tall flag reeds. He painted the loneliness and the smell of the salt-laden cold, the eternity and agelessness of marshes, the wild, living creatures, dawn flights, and frightened things taking to the air, and winged shadows at night hiding from the moon.

One November afternoon, three years after Rhayader had come to the Great Marsh, a child approached the lighthouse studio by means of the sea wall. In her arms she carried a burden.

She was no more than twelve, slender, dirty, nervous and timid as a bird, but beneath the grime as eerily beautiful as a marsh faery. She was pure Saxon, large-boned, fair, with a head to which her body was yet to grow, and deep-set, violet-coloured eyes.

She was desperately frightened of the ugly man she had come to see, for legend had already begun to gather about Rhayader, and the native wild-fowlers hated him for interfering with their sport.

But greater than her fear was the need of that which she bore. For locked in her child's heart was the knowledge, picked up somewhere in the swamp-land, that this ogre who lived in the lighthouse had magic that could heal injured things.

She had never seen Rhayader before and was close to fleeing in panic at the dark apparition that appeared at the studio door, drawn by her footsteps – the black head and beard, the sinister hump, and the crooked claw.

She stood there staring, poised like a disturbed marsh bird for instant flight.

But his voice was deep and kind when he spoke to her.

'What is it, child?'

She stood her ground, and then edged timidly forward. The thing she carried in her arms was a large white bird, and it was quite still. There were stains of blood on its whiteness and on her kirtle where she had held it to her.

The girl placed it in his arms. 'I found it, sir. It's hurted. Is it still alive?'

'Yes. Yes, I think so. Come in, child, come in.'

Rhayader went inside, bearing the bird, which he placed upon a table, where it moved feebly. Curiosity overcame fear. The girl followed and found herself in a room warmed by a coal fire, shining with many coloured pictures that covered the walls, and full of a strange but pleasant smell.

The bird fluttered. With his good hand Rhayader spread one of its immense white pinions. The end was beautifully tipped with black.

Rhayader looked and marvelled, and said: 'Child! where did you find it?'

'In t' marsh, sir, where fowlers had been. What — what is it, sir?'

'It's a snow goose from Canada. But how in all Heaven came it here?'

The name seemed to mean nothing to the little girl. Her deep violet eyes, shining out of the dirt on her thin face, were fixed with concern on the injured bird.

She said: 'Can 'ee heal it, sir?'

'Yes, yes,' said Rhayader. 'We will try. Come, you shall help me.'

There were scissors and bandages and splints on a shelf, and he was marvellously deft, even with the crooked claw that managed to hold things.

He said: 'Ah, she has been shot, poor thing. Her leg is broken, and the wing tip; but not badly. See, we will clip her primaries, so that we can bandage it, but in the spring the feathers will grow and she will be able to fly again. We'll bandage it close to her body, so that she cannot move it until it has set, and then make a splint for the poor leg.'

Her fear forgotten, the child watched, fascinated, as he worked, and all the more so because while he fixed a fine splint to the shattered leg he told her the most wonderful story.

The bird was a young one, no more than a year old. She was born in a northern land far, far across the seas, a land belonging to England. Flying to the south to escape the snow and ice and bitter cold, a great storm had seized her and whirled and buffeted her about. It was a truly terrible storm, stronger than her great wings, stronger than anything. For days and nights it held her in its grip and there was nothing she could do but fly before it. When finally it had blown itself out and her sure instincts took her south again, she was over a different land and surrounded by strange birds that she had never seen before. At last, exhausted by her ordeal, she had sunk to rest in a friendly green marsh, only to be met by the blast from the hunter's gun.

'A bitter reception for a visiting princess,' concluded Rhayader. 'We will call her *"La Princesse Perdue"*, the Lost Princess. And in a few days she will be feeling much better. See!' He reached into his pocket and produced a handful of grain. The snow goose opened its round yellow eyes and nibbled at it.

The child laughed with delight, and then suddenly caught her breath with alarm as the full import of where she was pressed in upon her, and without a word she turned and fled out of the door.

'Wait, wait!' cried Rhayader, and went to the entrance, where he stopped so that it framed his dark bulk. The girl was already fleeing down the sea wall, but she paused at his voice and looked back.

'What is your name, child?'

'Frith.'

'Eh?' said Rhayader. 'Fritha, I suppose. Where do you live?'

'Wi' t' fisherfolk at Wickaeldroth.' She gave the name the old Saxon pronunciation.

'Will you come back tomorrow, or the next day, to see how the Princess is getting along?'

She paused, and again Rhayader must have thought of the wild water birds caught motionless in that split second of alarm before they took to flight.

But her thin voice came back to him: 'Ay!'

And then she was gone, with her fair hair streaming out behind her.

The snow goose mended rapidly and by mid-winter was already limping about the enclosure with the wild pink-footed geese with which it associated, rather than the barnacles, and had learned to come to be fed at Rhayader's call. And the child Fritha, or Frith, was a frequent visitor. She had overcome her fear of Rhayader. Her imagination was captured by the presence of this strange white princess from a land far over the sea, a land that was all pink, as she knew from the map that Rhayader showed her, and on which they traced the stormy path of the lost bird from its home in Canada to the Great Marsh of Essex.

Then one June morning a group of late pink-feet, fat and well fed from the winter at the lighthouse, answered the stronger call of the breeding-grounds and rose lazily, climbing into the sky in ever widening circles. With them, her white body and black-tipped pinions shining in the spring sun, was the snow goose. It so happened that Frith was at the lighthouse. Her cry brought Rhayader running from the studio.

'Look! Look! The Princess! Be she going away?'

Rhayader stared into the sky at the climbing specks.

'Ay,' he said, unconsciously dropping into her manner of speech. 'The Princess is going home Listen! she is bidding us farewell.'

Out of the clear sky came the mournful barking of the pink-feet, and above it the higher, clearer note of the snow goose. The specks drifted northward, formed into a tiny v, diminished, and vanished.

With the departure of the snow goose ended the visits of Frith to the lighthouse. Rhayader learned all over again the meaning of the word 'loneliness'.

That summer, out of his memory, he painted a picture of a slender, grime-covered child, her fair hair blown by a November storm, who bore in her arms a wounded white bird.

In mid October the miracle occurred. Rhayader was in his enclosure, feeding his birds. A grey north-east wind was blowing and the land was sighing beneath the incoming tide. Above the sea and the wind noises he heard a clear, high note. He turned his eyes upward to the evening sky in time to see first an infinite speck, then a black-and-white pinioned dream that circled the lighthouse once, and finally a reality that dropped to earth in the pen and came waddling forward importantly to be fed, as though she had never been away. It was the snow goose. There was no mistaking her. Tears of joy came to Rhayader's eyes. Where had she been? Surely not home to Canada. No, she must have summered in Greenland or Spitzbergen with the pink-feet She had remembered and had returned.

When next Rhayader went into Chelmbury for supplies, he left a message with the postmistress — one that must have caused her much bewilderment. He said: 'Tell Frith, who lives with the fisherfolk at Wickael-droth, that the Lost Princess has returned.'

Three days later, Frith, taller, still tousled and unkempt, came shyly to the lighthouse to visit *La Princesse Perdue*.

Time passed. On the Great Marsh it was marked by the height of the tides, the slow march of the seasons, the passage of the birds, and, for Rhayader, by the arrival and departure of the snow goose.

The world outside boiled and seethed and rumbled with the eruption that was soon to break forth and come close to marking its destruction. But not yet did it touch upon Rhayader, or, for that matter, Frith. They had fallen into a curious natural rhythm, even as the child grew older. When the snow goose was at the lighthouse, then she came, too, to visit and learn many things from Rhayader. They sailed together in his speedy boat, that he handled so skilfully. They caught wildfowl for the ever-increasing colony, and built new pens and enclosures for them. From him she learned the lore of every wild bird, from gull to gyrfalcon, that flew the marshes.

She cooked for him sometimes, and even learned to mix his paints.

But when the snow goose returned to its summer home it was as though some kind of bar was up between them, and she did not come to the lighthouse. One year the bird did not return, and Rhayader was heartbroken. All things seemed to have ended for him. He painted furiously through the winter and the next summer, and never once saw the child. But in the fall the familiar cry once more rang from the sky, and the huge white bird, now at its full growth, dropped from the skies as mysteriously as it had departed. Joyously, Rhayader sailed his boat into Chelmbury and left his message with the postmistress.

Curiously, it was more than a month after he had left the message before Frith reappeared at the lighthouse, and Rhayader, with a shock, realised that she was a child no longer.

After the year in which the bird had remained away, its periods of absence grew shorter and shorter. It had grown so tame that it followed Rhayader about and even came into the studio while he was working.

In the spring of 1940 the birds migrated early from the Great Marsh. The world was on fire. The whine and roar of the bombers and the thudding explosions frightened them. The first day of May Frith and Rhayader stood shoulder to shoulder on the sea wall and watched the last of the unpinioned pink-feet and barnacle geese rise from their sanctuary; she, tall, slender, free as air and hauntingly beautiful; he, dark, grotesque, his massive bearded head raised to the sky, his glowing dark eyes watching the geese form their flight tracery.

'Look, Philip,' Frith said.

Rhayader followed her eyes. The snow goose had taken flight, her giant wings spread, but she was flying low, and once came quite close to them, so that for a moment the spreading black-tipped, white pinions seemed to caress them and they felt the rush of the bird's swift passage. Once, twice, she circled the lighthouse, then dropped to earth again in the enclosure with the pinioned geese and commenced to feed.

'She be'ent going,' said Frith, with marvel in her voice. The bird in its close passage seemed to have woven a kind of magic about her. 'The Princess be goin' t' stay.'

'Ay,' said Rhayader, and his voice was shaken too. 'She'll stay. She will never go away again. The Lost Princess is lost no more. This is her home now – of her own free will.'

The spell the bird had girt about her was broken, and Frith was suddenly conscious of the fact that she was frightened, and the things that frightened her were in Rhayader's eyes – the longing and the loneliness and the deep, welling, unspoken things that lay in and behind them as he turned them upon her.

His last words were repeating themselves in her head as though he had said them again: 'This is her home now – of her own free will.' The delicate tendrils of her instincts reached to him and carried to her the message of the things he could not speak because of what he felt himself to be, misshapen and grotesque. And where his voice might have soothed her, her fright grew greater at his silence and the power of the unspoken things between them. The woman in her bade her take flight from something that she was not yet capable of understanding.

Frith said: 'I – I must go. Goodbye. I be glad the – the Princess will stay. You'll not be so alone now.'

She turned and walked swiftly away, and his sadly spoken 'Goodbye, Frith,' was only a half-heard ghost of a sound borne to her ears above the rustling of the marsh grass. She was far away before she dared turn for a backward glance. He was still standing on the sea wall, a dark speck against the sky.

Her fear had stilled now. It had been replaced by something else, a queer sense of loss that made her stand quite still for a moment, so sharp was it. Then, more slowly, she continued on, away from the skyward-pointing finger of the lighthouse and the man beneath it.

It was a little more than three weeks before Frith
returned to the lighthouse. May was at its end, and the
day, too, in a long golden twilight that was giving way to
the silver of the moon already hanging in the eastern sky.

She told herself, as her steps took her thither, that she
must know whether the snow goose had really stayed, as
Rhayader said it would. Perhaps it had flown away, after
all. But her firm tread on the sea wall was full of
eagerness and sometimes unconsciously she found herself hurrying.

Frith saw the yellow light of Rhayader's lantern down
by his little wharf, and she found him there. His sailboat
was rocking gently on a flooding tide and he was loading
supplies into her – water and food and bottles of brandy,
gear, and a spare sail. When he turned to the sound of
her coming, she saw that he was pale, but that his dark
eyes, usually so kind and placid, were glowing with
excitement, and he was breathing heavily from his
exertions.

Sudden alarm seized Frith. The snow goose was
forgotten. 'Philip! Ye be goin' away?'

Rhayader paused in his work to greet her, and there
was something in his face, a glow and a look, that she had
never seen there before.

'Frith! I am glad you came. Yes, I must go away. A
little trip. I will come back.' His usually kindly voice was
hoarse with what was suppressed inside him.

Frith asked: 'Where must ye go?'

Words came tumbling from Rhayader now. He must go to Dunkirk. A hundred miles across the Channel. A British army was trapped there on the sands, awaiting destruction at the hands of the advancing Germans. The port was in flames, the position hopeless. He had heard it in the village when he had gone for supplies. Men were putting out from Chelmbury in answer to the government's call, every tug and fishing boat or power launch that could propel itself was heading across the Channel to haul the men off the beaches to the transports and destroyers that could not reach the shallows, to rescue as many as possible from the Germans' fire.

Frith listened and felt her heart dying within her. He was saying that he would sail the Channel in his little boat. It could take six men at a time; in a pinch, seven. He could make many trips from the beaches to the transports.

The girl was young, primitive, inarticulate. She did not understand war, or what had happened in France, or the meaning of the trapped army, but the blood within her told her that here was danger.

'Philip! Must 'ee go? You'll not come back. Why must it be 'ee?'

The fever seemed to have gone from Rhayader's soul with the first rush of words, and he explained it to her in terms that she could understand.

He said: 'Men are huddled on the beaches like hunted birds, Frith, like the wounded and hunted birds we used to find and bring to sanctuary. Over them fly the steel peregrines, hawks, and gyrfalcons, and they have no shelter from these iron birds of prey. They are lost and storm-driven and harried, like the *Princesse Perdue* you found and brought to me out of the marshes many years ago, and we healed her. They need help, my dear, as our wild creatures have needed help, and that is why I must go. It is something that I can do. Yes, I can. For once — for once I can be a man and play my part.'

Frith stared at Rhayader. He had changed so. For the first time she saw that he was no longer ugly or misshapen or grotesque, but very beautiful. Things were turmoiling in her own soul, crying to be said, and she did not know how to say them.

'I'll come with 'ee! Philip.'

Rhayader shook his head. 'Your place in the boat would cause a soldier to be left behind, and another, and another. I must go alone.'

He donned rubber coat and boots and took to his boat. He waved and called back: 'Goodbye! Will you look after the birds until I return, Frith?'

Frith's hand came up, but only half, to wave too. 'God speed you,' she said, but gave it the Saxon turn. 'I will take care of t' birds. God-speed, Philip.'

It was night now, bright with moon fragment and stars and northern glow. Frith stood on the sea wall and watched the sail gliding down the swollen estuary. Suddenly from the darkness behind her there came a rush of wings, and something swept past her into the air. In the night light she saw the flash of white wings, black-tipped, and the thrust-forward head of the snow goose.

It rose and cruised over the lighthouse once and then headed down the winding creek where Rhayader's sail was slanting in the gaining breeze, and flew above him in slow, wide circles.

White sail and white bird were visible for a long time.

'Watch o'er him. Watch o'er him,' Frith whispered. When they were both out of sight at last, she turned and walked slowly, with bent head, back to the empty lighthouse.

Now the story becomes fragmentary, and one of these fragments is in the words of the men on leave who told it in the public room of the Crown and Arrow, an East Chapel pub.

'A goose, a bloomin' goose, so 'elp me,' said Private Potton, of His Majesty's London Rifles.

'Garn,' said a bandy-legged artilleryman.

'A goose it was. Jock, 'ere, seed it same as me. It come flyin' down outa the muck an' stink an' smoke of Dunkirk that was over'ead. It was white, wiv black on its wings, an' it circles us like a bloomin' dive bomber. Jock, 'ere, 'e sez: "We're done for. It's the hangel of death a-come for us."

' "Garn," Hi sez, "it's a ruddy goose, come over from 'ome wiv a message from Churchill, an' 'ow are we henjoying the bloomin' bathing. It's a omen, that's what it is, a bloody omen. We'll get out of this yet, me lad."

'We was roostin' on the beach between Dunkirk an' Lapanny, like a lot o' bloomin' pigeons on Victoria Hembankment, waitin' for Jerry to pot us. 'E potted us good too. 'E was be'ind us an' flankin' us an' above us. 'E give us shrapnel and 'e give us H.E., an' 'e peppers us from the bloomin' hatmosphere with Jittersmiths.

'An' offshore is the *Kentish Maid,* a ruddy hexcursion scow wot Hi've taken many a trip on out of Margate in the summer, for two-and-six, waiting to take us off, 'arf a mile out from the bloomin' shallows.

'While we are lyin' there on the beach, done in an' cursin' becos there ain't no way to get out to the boat, a Stuka dives on 'er, an' 'is bombs drop alongside of 'er, throwin' up water like the bloomin' fountains in the palace gardens; a reg'lar display it was.

'Then a destroyer come up an' says: "No, ye don't" to the Stuka with ack-acks and pom-poms, but another Jerry dives on the destroyer, an' 'its 'er. Coo, did she go up! She burned before she sunk, an' the smoke an' the stink come driftin' inshore, all yellow an' black, an' out of it comes this bloomin' goose, a-circlin' around us trapped on the beach.

'An' then around a bend 'e comes in a bloody little sailboat, sailing along as cool as you please, like a

[23]

bloomin' toff out for a pleasure spin on a Sunday hafternoon at 'Enley.'

' 'Oo comes?' inquired a civilian.

' 'Im! 'Im that saved a lot of us. 'E sailed clean through a boil of machine-gun bullets from a Jerry in a Jittersmith wot was strafin' – a Ramsgate motor-boat wot 'ad tried to take us off 'ad been sunk there 'arf an hour ago – the water was all frothin' with shell splashes an' bullets, but 'e didn't give it no mind, 'e didn't. 'E didn't 'ave no petrol to burn or hexplode, an' he sailed in between the shells.

'Into the shallows 'e come out of the black smoke of the burnin' destroyer, a little dark man wiv a beard, a bloomin' claw for a 'and, an' a 'ump on 'is back.

' 'E 'ad a rope in 'is teeth that was shinin' white out of 'is black beard, 'is good 'and on the tiller an' the crooked one beckonin' to us to come. An' over'ead, around and around, flied the ruddy goose.

'Jock, 'ere, says: "Lawk, it's all over now. It's the bloody devil come for us 'imself. Hi must 'ave been struck an' don't know it."

' "Garn," I sez, "it's more like the good Lord, 'e looks to me, than any bloomin' devil." 'E did, too, like the pictures from the Sunday-school books, wiv 'is white face and dark eyes an' beard an' all, and 'is bloomin' boat.

' "Hi can taken seven at a time," 'e sings out when 'e's in close.

'Our horfficer shouts: "Good man! . . . You seven nearest, get in."

'We waded out to where 'e was. Hi was that weary Hi couldn't climb over the side, but 'e takes me by the collar of me tunic an' pulls, wiv a "In ye go, lad. Come on. Next man."

'An' in Hi went. Coo, 'e was strong, 'e was. Then 'e sets 'is sail, part of wot looks like a bloomin' sieve from machine-gun bullets, shouts: "Keep down in the bottom of the boat, boys, in case we meet any of yer friends," and we're off, 'im sittin' in the stern wiv 'is rope in 'is teeth, another in 'is crooked claw, an' 'is right 'and on the tiller, a-steerin' an' sailin' through the spray of the shells thrown by a land battery somewhere back of the coast. An' the bloomin' goose is flyin' around and around, 'onking above the wind and the row Jerry was makin', like a bloomin' Morris on Winchester by-pass.

' "Hi told you yon goose was a omen," Hi sez to Jock. "Look at 'im there, a bloomin' hangel of mercy."

' 'Im at the tiller just looks up at the goose, wiv the rope in 'is teeth, an' grins at 'er like 'e knows 'er a lifetime.

' 'E brung us out to the *Kentish Maid* and turns around and goes back for another load. 'E made trips all afternoon an' all night, too, because the bloody light of Dunkirk burning was bright enough to see by. Hi don't know 'ow many trips 'e made, but 'im an' a nobby Thames Yacht Club motorboat an' a big lifeboat from

Poole that come along brought off all there was of us on that particular stretch of hell, without the loss of a man.

'We sailed when the last man was off, an' there was more than seven hunder' of us haboard a boat built to take two hunder'. 'E was still there when we left, an' 'e waved us good-bye and sails off towards Dunkirk, and the bird wiv 'im. Blimey, it was queer to see that ruddy big goose flyin' around 'is boat, lit up by the fires like a white hangel against the smoke.

'A Stuka 'ad another go at us, 'arfway across, but 'e'd been stayin' up late nights, an' missed. By mornin' we was safe 'ome.

'Hi never did find out what become of 'im, or 'oo 'e was — 'im wiv the 'ump an' 'is little sail-boat. A bloody good man 'e was, that chap.'

'Coo,' said the artilleryman. 'A ruddy big goose. Whatcher know?'

In an officers' club in Brook Street, a retired naval officer, sixty-five years old, Commander Keith Brill-Oudener, was telling of his experiences during the evacuation of Dunkirk. Called out of bed at four o'clock in the morning, he had captained a lopsided Limehouse tug across the Channel, towing a string of Thames barges, which he brought back four times loaded with soldiers. On his last trip he came in with her funnel shot away and a hole in her side. But he got her back to Dover.

A naval-reserve officer, who had two Brixham trawlers and a Yarmouth drifter blasted out from under him in the last four days of the evacuation, said: 'Did you run across that queer sort of legend about a wild goose? It was all up and down the beaches. You know how those things spring up. Some of the men I brought back were talking about it. It was supposed to have appeared at intervals the last days between Dunkirk and La Panne. If you saw it, you were eventually saved. That sort of thing.'

'H'm'm'm,' said Brill-Oudener, 'a wild goose. I saw a tame one. Dashed strange experience. Tragic in a way, too. And lucky for us. Tell you about it. Third trip back. Toward six o'clock we sighted a derelict small boat. Seemed to be a chap or a body in her. And a bird perched on the rail.

'We changed our course when we got nearer, and went over for a look-see. By Gad, it was a chap. Or had been, poor fellow. Machine-gunned, you know. Badly. Face down in the water. Bird was a goose, a tame one.

'We drifted close, but when one of our chaps reached over, the bird hissed at him and struck at him with her wings. Couldn't drive it off. Suddenly young Kettering, who was with me, gave a hail and pointed to starboard. Big mine floating by. One of Jerry's beauties. If we'd kept on our course we'd have piled right into it. Ugh!

Head on. We let it get a hundred yards astern of the last barge, and the men blew it up with rifle-fire.

'When we turned our attention to the derelict again, she was gone. Sunk. Concussion, you know. Chap with her. He must have been lashed to her. The bird had got up and was circling. Three times, like a plane saluting. Dashed queer feeling. Then she flew off to the west. Lucky thing for us we went over to have a look, eh? Odd that you should mention a goose.'

Fritha remained alone at the little lighthouse on the Great Marsh, taking care of the pinioned birds, waiting for she knew not what. The first days she haunted the sea wall, watching; though she knew it was useless. Later she roamed through the storerooms of the lighthouse building with their stacks of canvases on which Rhayader had captured every mood and light of the desolate country and the wondrous, graceful, feathered things that inhabited it.

Among them she found the picture that Rhayader had painted of her from memory so many years ago, when she was still a child, and had stood, windblown and timid, at his threshold, hugging an injured bird to her.

The picture and the things she saw in it stirred her as nothing ever had before, for much of Rhayader's soul had gone into it. Strangely, it was the only time he had painted the snow goose, the lost wild creature, storm-driven from another land, that to each had brought a friend, and which, in the end, returned to her with the message that she would never see him again.

Long before the snow goose had come dropping out of a crimsoned eastern sky to circle the lighthouse in a last farewell, Fritha, from the ancient powers of the blood that was in her, knew that Rhayader would not return.

And so, when one sunset she heard the high-pitched, well-remembered note cried from the heavens, it brought no instant of false hope to her heart. This moment, it seemed, she had lived before many times.

She came running to the sea wall and turned her eyes, not towards the distant Channel whence a sail might come, but to the sky from whose flaming arches plummeted the snow goose. Then the sight, the sound, and the solitude surrounding broke the dam within her and released the surging, overwhelming truth of her love, let it well forth in tears.

Wild spirit called to wild spirit, and she seemed to be flying with the great bird, soaring with it in the evening sky and hearkening to Rhayader's message.

Sky and earth were trembling with it and filled her beyond the bearing of it. 'Frith! Fritha! Frith, my love. Goodbye, my love.' The white pinions, black-tipped, were beating it out upon her heart, and her heart was answering: 'Philip, I love 'ee.'

For a moment Frith thought the snow goose was going to land in the old enclosure, as the pinioned geese set up a welcoming gabble. But it only skimmed low, then soared up again, flew in a wide, graceful spiral once around the old light, and then began to climb.

Watching it, Frith saw no longer the snow goose but the soul of Rhayader taking farewell of her before departing for ever.

She was no longer flying with it, but earth-bound. She stretched her arms up into the sky and stood on tiptoes, reaching, and cried: 'God-speed, God-speed, Philip!'

Frith's tears were stilled. She stood watching silently long after the goose had vanished. Then she went into the lighthouse and secured the picture that Rhayader had painted of her. Hugging it to her breast, she wended her way homeward along the old sea wall.

Each night, for many weeks thereafter, Frith came to the lighthouse and fed the pinioned birds. Then one early morning a German pilot on a dawn raid mistook the old abandoned light for an active military objective, dived on to it, a screaming steel hawk, and blew it and all it contained into oblivion.

That evening when Fritha came, the sea had moved in through the breached walls and covered it over. Nothing was left to break the utter desolation. No marsh fowl had dared to return. Only the frightless gulls wheeled and soared and mewed their plaint over the place where it had been.

THE SMALL MIRACLE

To
ST FRANCIS
a man among
saints

The beautiful setting of Assisi is clearly essential for the purposes of this story. But the characters exist only in the imagination of the author and are not based upon any real persons. They are delineated as they are for purely literary reasons.

APPROACHING ASSISI VIA THE chalky, dusty road that twists its way up Monte Subasio, now revealing, now concealing the exquisite little town, as it winds its way through olive and cypress groves, you eventually reach a division where your choice lies between an upper and a lower route.

If you select the latter, you soon find yourself entering Assisi through the twelfth-century archway of the denticulated door of St Francis. But if, seduced by the clear air, the wish to mount even closer to the canopy of blue Italian sky and expose still more of the delectable view of the rich Umbrian valley below, you choose the upper way, you and your vehicle eventually become inextricably entangled in the welter of humanity, oxen, goats, bawling calves, mules, fowl, children, pigs, booths and carts gathered at the market place outside the walls.

It is here you would be most likely to encounter Pepino, with his donkey Violetta, hard at work, turning his hand to anything whereby a small boy and a strong, willing beast of burden could win for themselves the crumpled ten and twenty lire notes needed to buy food and pay for lodging in the barn of Niccolo the stableman.

Pepino and Violetta were everything to each other. They were a familiar sight about Assisi and its immediate environs – the thin brown boy, ragged and barefooted, with the enormous dark eyes, large ears, and close-cropped, upstanding hair, and the dust-coloured little donkey with the Mona Lisa smile.

Pepino was ten years old and an orphan, his father, mother and near relatives having been killed in the war. In self-reliance, wisdom and demeanour he was, of course, much older, a circumstance aided by his independence, for Pepino was an unusual orphan in that having a heritage he need rely on no one. Pepino's heritage was Violetta.

She was a good, useful and docile donkey, alike as any other with friendly, gentle eyes, soft taupe-coloured muzzle, and long, pointed brown ears, with one exception that distinguished her. Violetta had a curious expression about the corners of her mouth, as though she were smiling gently over something that amused or pleased her. Thus, no matter what kind of work, or how much she was asked to do, she always appeared to be performing it with a smile of quiet satisfaction. The combination of Pepino's dark lustrous eyes and Violetta's smile was so harmonious that people favoured them and they were able not only to earn enough for their keep but, aided and advised by Father Damico, the priest of their parish, to save a little as well.

There were all kinds of things they could do — carry loads of wood or water, deliver purchases carried in the panniers that thumped against Violetta's sides, hire out to help pull a cart mired in the mud, aid in the olive harvest, and even, occasionally, help some citizen who was too encumbered with wine to reach his home on foot, by means of a four-footed taxi with Pepino walking beside to see that the drunkard did not fall off.

But this was not the only reason for the love that existed between boy and donkey, for Violetta was more than just the means of his livelihood. She was mother to him, and father, brother, playmate, companion, and comfort. At night in the straw of Niccolo's stable, Pepino slept curled up close to her when it was cold, his head pillowed on her neck.

Since the mountainside was a rough world for a small boy, he was sometimes beaten or injured, and then he could creep to her for comfort and Violetta would gently nuzzle his bruises. When there was joy in his heart, he shouted songs into her waving ears; when he was lonely and hurt, he could lean his head against her soft, warm flank and cry out his tears.

On his part, he fed her, watered her, searched her for ticks and parasites, picked stones from her hoofs, scratched and groomed and curried her, lavished affection on her particularly when they were alone, while in public he never beat her with the donkey stick more than was necessary. For this treatment Violetta made a god of Pepino, and repaid him with loyalty, obedience and affection.

Thus, when one day in the early spring Violetta fell ill, it was the most serious thing that had ever happened to Pepino. It began first with an unusual lethargy that would respond neither to stick nor caresses, nor the young, strident voice urging her on. Later Pepino observed other symptoms and a visible loss of weight. Her ribs, once so well padded, began to show through her sides. But most distressing, either through a change in the conformation of her head, due to growing thinner, or because of the distress of the illness, Violetta lost her enchanting and lovable smile.

Drawing upon his carefully hoarded reserves of lire notes and parting with several of the impressive denomination of a hundred, Pepino called in Dr Bartoli, the vet.

The vet examined her in good faith, dosed her, and tried his best; but she did not improve and, instead, continued to lose weight and grow weaker. He hummed and hawed then and said, 'Well, now, it is hard to say. It might be one thing, such as the bite of a fly new to this district, or another, such as a germ settling in the intestine.' Either way, how could one tell? There had been a similar case in Foligno and another in a far-away town. He recommended resting the beast and feeding her lightly. If the illness passed from her and God willed, she might live. Otherwise, she would surely die and there would be an end to her suffering.

After he had gone away, Pepino put his cropped head on Violetta's heaving flank and wept unrestrainedly. But then, when the storm, induced by the fear of losing his only companion in the world, had subsided, he knew what he must do. If there was no help for Violetta on earth, the appeal must be registered above. His plan was nothing less than to take Violetta into the crypt beneath the lower church of the Basilica of St Francis, where rested the remains of the Saint who had so dearly loved God's creations, including all the feathered and the four-footed brothers and sisters who served Him. There he would beg St Francis to heal her. Pepino had no doubt that the Saint would do so when he saw Violetta.

These things Pepino knew from Father Damico, who had a way of talking about St Francis as though he were a living person who might still be encountered in his frayed cowl, bound with a hemp cord at the middle, merely by turning a corner of the main square in Assisi or by walking down one of the narrow, cobbled streets.

And besides, there was a precedent. Giani, his friend, the son of Niccolo the stableman, had taken his sick kitten into the crypt and asked St Francis to heal her, and the cat had got well – at least half well, anyway, for her hind legs still dragged a little; but at least she had not died. Pepino felt that if Violetta were to die, it would be the end of everything for him.

Thereupon, with considerable difficulty, he per-suaded the sick and shaky donkey to rise, and with urgings and caresses and minimum use of the stick drove her through the crooked streets of Assisi and up the hill to the Basilica of St Francis. At the beautiful twin portal of the lower church he respectfully asked Fra Bernard, who was on duty there, for permission to take Violetta down to St Francis, so that she might be made well again.

Fra Bernard was a new monk, and, calling Pepino a young and impious scoundrel, ordered him and his donkey to be off. It was strictly forbidden to bring livestock into the church, and even to think of taking an ass into the crypt of St Francis was a desecration. And besides, how did he imagine she would get down there when the narrow, winding staircase was barely wide enough to accommodate humans in single file, much less four-footed animals? Pepino must be a fool as well as a shiftless rascal.

As ordered, Pepino retreated from the portal, his arm about Violetta's neck, and bethought himself of what he must do next to succeed in his purpose, for while he was disappointed at the rebuff he had received, he was not at all discouraged.

Despite the tragedy that had struck Pepino's early life and robbed him of his family, he really considered himself a most fortunate boy, compared with many, since he had acquired not only a heritage to aid him in earning a living but also an important precept by which to live.

This maxim, the golden key to success, had been left with Pepino, together with bars of chocolate, chewing gum, peanut brittle, soap, and other delights, by a corporal in the United States Army who had, in the six months he had been stationed in the vicinity of Assisi, been Pepino's demigod and hero. His name was Francis Xavier O'Halloran, and what he told Pepino before he departed out of this life for ever was, 'If you want to get ahead in this world, kid, don't never take no for an answer. Get it?' Pepino never forgot this important advice.

He thought now that his next step was clear; nevertheless, he went first to his friend and adviser, Father Damico, for confirmation.

Father Damico, who had a broad head, lustrous eyes, and shoulders shaped as though they had been especially designed to support the burdens laid upon them by his parishioners, said, 'You are within your rights, my son, in taking your request to the lay Supervisor and it lies within his power to grant or refuse it.'

There was no malice in the encouragement he thus gave Pepino, but it was also true that he was not loath to see the Supervisor brought face to face with an example of pure and innocent faith. For in his private opinion that worthy man was too much concerned with the twin churches that formed the Basilica and the crypt as a tourist attraction. He, Father Damico, could not see why the child should not have his wish, but, of course, it was out of his jurisdiction. He was, however, curious about how the Supervisor would react, even though he thought he knew in advance.

However, he did not impart his fears to Pepino and merely called after him as he was leaving, 'And if the little one cannot be got in from above, there is another entrance from below, through the old church, only it has been walled up for a hundred years. But it could be opened. You might remind the Supervisor when you see him. He knows where it is.'

Pepino thanked him and went back alone to the Basilica and the monastery attached to it and asked permission to see the Supervisor.

This personage was an accessible man, and even though he was engaged in a conversation with the Bishop, he sent for Pepino, who walked into the cloister gardens where he waited respectfully for the two great men to finish.

The two dignitaries were walking up and down, and Pepino wished it were the Bishop who was to say yea or nay to his request, as he looked the kindlier of the two, the Supervisor appearing to have more the expression of a merchant. The boy pricked up his ears, because, as it happened, so they were speaking of St Francis, and the Bishop was just remarking with a sigh, 'He has been gone too long from this earth. The lesson of his life is plain to all who can read. But who in these times will pause to do so?'

The Supervisor said, 'His tomb in the crypt attracts many to Assisi. But in a Holy Year, relics are even better. If we but had the tongue of the Saint, or a lock of his hair, or a fingernail.'

The Bishop had a far-away look in his eyes, and he was shaking his head gently. 'It is a message we are in need of, my dear Supervisor, a message from a great heart that would speak to us across the gap of seven centuries to remind us of The Way.' And here he paused and coughed, for he was a polite man and noticed that Pepino was waiting.

The Supervisor turned also and said, 'Ah yes, my son, what is it that I can do for you?'

Pepino said, 'Please, sir, my donkey Violetta is very sick. Dr Bartoli has said he can do nothing more and perhaps she will die. Please, I would like permission to take her into the tomb of St Francis and ask him to cure her. He loved all animals, and particularly little donkeys. I am sure he will make her well.'

The Supervisor looked shocked. 'A donkey. In the crypt. However did you come to that idea?'

Pepino explained about Giani and his sick kitten, while the Bishop turned away to hide a smile.

But the Supervisor was not smiling. He asked, 'How did this Giani succeed in smuggling a kitten into the tomb?'

Since it was all over, Pepino saw no reason for not telling, and replied, 'Under his coat, sir.'

The Supervisor made a mental note to warn the brothers to keep a sharper eye out for small boys or other persons with suspicious-looking lumps under their outer clothing.

'Of course we can have no such goings-on,' he said. 'The next thing you know, everyone would be coming, bringing a sick dog, or an ox, or a goat, or even a pig. And then where should we end up? A veritable sty.'

'But, sir,' Pepino pleaded, 'no one need know. We would come and go so very quickly.'

The Supervisor's mind played. There was something touching about the boy – the bullet head, the enormous eyes, the jug-handle ears. And yet, what if he permitted it and the donkey then died, as seemed most likely if Dr Bartoli had said there was no further hope? Word was sure to get about, and the shrine would suffer from it. He wondered what the Bishop was thinking and how *he* would solve the problem.

He equivocated: 'And besides, even if we were to allow it, you would never be able to get your donkey around the turn at the bottom of the stairs. So, you see, it is quite impossible.'

'But there is another entrance,' Pepino said. 'From the old church. It has not been used for a long time, but it could be opened just this once – couldn't it?'

The Supervisor was indignant. 'What are you saying –

destroy church property? The entrance has been walled up for over a century, ever since the new crypt was built.'

The Bishop thought he saw a way out and said gently to the boy, 'Why do you not go home and pray to St Francis to assist you? If you open your heart to him and have faith, he will surely hear you.'

'But it wouldn't be the same,' Pepino cried, and his voice was shaking with the sobs that wanted to come. 'I must take her where St Francis can see her. She isn't like any other old donkey — Violetta has the sweetest smile. She does not smile any more since she has been so ill. But perhaps she would, just once more for St Francis. And when he saw it he would not be able to resist her, and he would make her well. I know he would!'

The Supervisor knew his ground now. He said, 'I am sorry, my son, but the answer is no.'

But even through his despair and the bitter tears he shed as he went away, Pepino knew that if Violetta was to live he must not take no for an answer.

'Who is there, then?' Pepino asked of Father Damico later. 'Who is above the Supervisor and my lord the Bishop who might tell them to let me take Violetta into the crypt?'

Father Damico's stomach felt cold as he thought of the dizzying hierarchy between Assisi and Rome. Nevertheless, he explained as best he could, concluding with, 'And at the top is His Holiness the Pope himself.

Surely his heart would be touched by what has happened if you were able to tell him, for he is a great and good man. But he is busy with important weighty affairs, Pepino, and it would be impossible for him to see you.'

Pepino went back to Niccolo's stable, where he ministered to Violetta, fed and watered her and rubbed her muzzle a hundred times. Then he withdrew his money from the stone jar buried under the straw and counted it. He had almost three hundred lire. A hundred of it he set aside and promised to his friend Giani if he would look after Violetta, while Pepino was gone, as if she were his own. Then he patted her once more, brushed away the tears that had started again at the sight of how thin she was, put on his jacket, and went out on the high road, where, using his thumb as he had learned from Corporal Francis Xavier O'Halloran, he got a lift in a lorry going to Foligno and the main road. He was on his way to Rome to see the Holy Father.

Never had any small boy looked quite so infinitesimal and forlorn as Pepino standing in the boundless and almost deserted, since it was early in the morning, St Peter's Square. Everything towered over him – the massive dome of St Peter's, the obelisk of Caligula, the Bernini colonnades. Everything contrived to make him look pinched and miserable in his bare feet, torn trousers, and ragged jacket. Never was a boy more overpowered, lonely, and frightened, or carried a greater burden of unhappiness in his heart.

For now that he was at last in Rome, the gigantic proportions of the buildings and monuments, their awe and majesty, began to sap his courage, and he seemed to have a glimpse into the utter futility and hopelessness of his mission. And then there would arise in his mind a picture of the sad little donkey who did not smile any more, her heaving flanks and clouded eyes, and who would surely die unless he could find help for her. It was thoughts like these that enabled him finally to cross the piazza and timidly approach one of the smaller side entrances to the Vatican.

The Swiss guard, in his slashed red, yellow, and blue uniform, with his long halberd, looked enormous and forbidding. Nevertheless, Pepino edged up to him and said, 'Please, will you take me to see the Pope? I wish to speak to him about my donkey Violetta, who is very ill and may die unless the Pope will help me.'

The guard smiled, not unkindly, for he was used to these ignorant and innocent requests, and the fact that it came from a dirty ragged little boy, with eyes like ink pools and a round head from which the ears stood out like the handles on a cream jug, made it all the more harmless. But, nevertheless, he was shaking his head as he smiled and then said that His Holiness was a very busy man and could not be seen. And the guard grounded his halberd with a thud and let it fall slantwise across the door to show that he meant business.

Pepino backed away. What good was his precept in the face of such power and majesty? And yet the memory of what Corporal O'Halloran had said told him that he must return to the Vatican yet once again.

At the side of the piazza he saw an old woman sitting under an umbrella, selling little bouquets and nosegays of spring flowers – daffodils and jonquils, snowdrops and white narcissus, Parma violets and lilies of the valley, vari-coloured carnations, pansies, and tiny sweetheart roses. Some of the people visiting St Peter's liked to place these on the altar of their favourite saint. The flowers were crisp and fresh from the market, and many of them had glistening drops of water still clinging to their petals.

Looking at them made Pepino think of home and Father Damico and what he had said of the love St Francis had for flowers. Father Damico had the gift of making everything he thought and said sound like poetry. And Pepino came to the conclusion that if St Francis, who had been a holy man, had been so fond of flowers, perhaps the Pope, who according to his position was even holier, would love them, too.

For fifty lire he bought a tiny bouquet in which a spray of lilies of the valley rose from a bed of dark violets and small red roses crowded next to yellow pansies all tied about with leaf and feather fern and paper lace.

From a stall where postcards and souvenirs were sold, he begged pencil and paper, and laboriously composed a note:

> *Dear and most sacred Holy Father: These flowers are for you. Please let me see you and tell you about my donkey Violetta who is dying, and they will not let me take her to see St Francis so that he may cure her. I live in the town of Assisi, but I have come all the way here to see you.*
>
> *Your loving Pepino.*

Thereupon, he returned to the door, placed the bouquet and the note in the hand of the Swiss guard, and begged, 'Please take these up to the Pope. I am sure he will see me when he receives the flowers and reads what I have written.'

The guard had not expected this. The child and the flowers had suddenly placed him in a dilemma from which he could not extricate himself in the presence of those large and trusting eyes. However, he was not without experience in handling such matters. He had only to place a colleague at his post, go to the Guard Room, throw the flowers and the note into the wastepaper basket, absent himself for a sufficient length of time, and then return to tell the boy that His Holiness thanked him for the gift of the flowers and regretted that press of important business made it impossible for him to grant him an audience.

[49]

This little subterfuge the guard put into motion at once; but when he came to completing the next-to-last act in it, he found to his amazement that somehow he could not bring himself to do it. There was the wastepaper basket, yawning to receive the offering, but the little nosegay seemed to be glued to his fingers. How gay, sweet, and cool the flowers were. What thoughts they brought to his mind of spring in the green valleys of his far-off canton of Luzern. He saw again the snow-capped mountains of his youth, the little gingerbread houses, the grey, soft-eyed cattle grazing in the blossom-carpeted meadows, and he heard the heart-warming tinkling of their bells.

Dazed by what had happened to him, he left the Guard Room and wandered through the corridors, for he did not know where to go or what to do with his burden. He was eventually encountered by a busy little Monsignor, one of the vast army of clerks and secretaries employed in the Vatican, who paused, astonished at the sight of the burly guard helplessly contemplating a tiny posy.

And thus occurred the minor miracle whereby Pepino's plea and offering crossed the boundary in the palace that divided the mundane from the spiritual, the lay from the ecclesiastical.

For to the great relief of the guard, the Monsignor

took over the burning articles that he had been unable to relinquish; and this priest they touched, too, as it is the peculiar power of flowers that while they are universal and spread their species over the world, they invoke in each beholder the dearest and most cherished memories.

In this manner, the little bouquet passed on and upward from hand to hand, pausing briefly in the possession of the clerk of the Apostolic Chamber, the Privy Almoner, the Papal Sacristan, the Master of the Sacred Palaces, the Papal Chamberlain. The dew vanished from the flowers; they began to lose their freshness and to wilt, passing from hand to hand. And yet they retained their magic, the message of love and memories that rendered it impossible for any of these intermediaries to dispose of them.

Eventually, then, they were deposited with the missive that accompanied them on the desk of the man for whom they had been destined. He read the note and then sat there silently contemplating the blossoms. He closed his eyes for a moment, the better to entertain the picture that arose in his mind of himself as a small Roman boy taken on a Sunday into the Alban Hills, where for the first time he saw violets growing wild.

When he opened his eyes at last, he said to his secretary, 'Let the child be brought here. I will see him.'

Thus it was that Pepino at last came into the presence of the Pope, seated at his desk in his office. Perched on the edge of a chair next to him, Pepino told the whole story about Violetta, his need to take her into the tomb of St Francis, about the Supervisor who was preventing him, and all about Father Damico, too, and the second entrance to the crypt, Violetta's smile, and his love for her – everything, in fact, that was in his heart and that now poured forth to the sympathetic man sitting quietly behind the desk.

And when, at the end of half an hour, he was ushered from the presence, he was quite sure he was the happiest boy in the world. For he had not only the blessing of the Pope, but also, under his jacket, two letters, one addressed to the lay Supervisor of the Monastery of Assisi and the other to Father Damico. No longer did he feel small and overwhelmed when he stepped out on to the square again past the astonished but delighted Swiss guard. He felt as though he could give one leap and a bound and fly back to his Violetta's side.

Nevertheless, he had to give heed to the more practical side of transportation. He enquired his way to a bus that took him to where the Via Flaminia became a country road stretching to the north, then plied his thumb backed by his eloquent eyes, and before nightfall of that day, with good luck, was home in Assisi.

After a visit to Violetta had assured him that she had been well looked after and at least was no worse than she had been before his departure, Pepino proudly went to Father Damico and presented his letters as he had been instructed to do.

The Father fingered the envelope for the Supervisor and then, with a great surge of warmth and happiness, read the one addressed to himself. He said to Pepino, 'Tomorrow we will take the Supervisor's letter to him. He will summon masons and the old door will be broken down and you will be able to take Violetta into the tomb and pray there for her recovery. The Pope himself has approved it.'

The Pope, of course, had not written the letters personally. They had been composed with considerable delight and satisfaction by the Cardinal-Secretary, backed by Papal authority, who said in his missive to Father Damico:

> Surely the Supervisor must know that in his lifetime the blessed St Francis was accompanied to chapel by a little lamb that used to follow him about Assisi. Is an asinus any less created by God because his coat is rougher and his ears longer?

And he wrote also of another matter, which Father Damico imparted to Pepino in his own way.

He said, 'Pepino, there is something you must understand before we go to see the Abbot. It is your hope that because of your faith in St Francis he will help you and heal your donkey. But had you thought, perhaps, that he who dearly cared for all of God's creatures might come to love Violetta so greatly that he would wish to have her at his side in Eternity?'

[53]

A cold terror gripped Pepino as he listened. He managed to say, 'No, Father, I had not thought — '

The priest continued: 'Will you go to the crypt only to ask, Pepino, or will you also, if necessary, be prepared to give?'

Everything in Pepino cried out against the possibility of losing Violetta, even to someone as beloved as St Francis. Yet when he raised his stricken face and looked into the lustrous eyes of Father Damico, there was something in their depths that gave him the courage to whisper, 'I will give – if I must. But, oh, I hope he will let her stay with me just a little longer.'

The clink of the stonemason's pick rang again and again through the vaulted chamber of the lower church, where the walled-up door of the passageway leading to the crypt was being removed. Nearby waited the Supervisor and his friend the Bishop, Father Damico, and Pepino, large-eyed, pale, and silent. The boy kept his arms about the neck of Violetta and his face pressed to hers. The little donkey was very shaky on her legs and could barely stand.

The Supervisor watched humbly and impassively while broken bricks and clods of mortar fell as the breach widened and the freed current of air from the passage swirled the plaster dust in clouds. He was a just man for all his weakness, and had invited the Bishop to witness his rebuke.

A portion of the wall proved obstinate. The mason attacked the archway at the side to weaken its support. Then the loosened masonry began to tumble again. A narrow passageway was effected, and through the opening they could see the distant flicker of the candles placed at the altar wherein rested the remains of St. Francis.

Pepino stirred towards the opening. Or was it Violetta who had moved nervously, frightened by the unaccustomed place and noises? Father Damico said, 'Wait,' and Pepino held her; but the donkey's uncertain feet slipped on the rubble and then lashed out in panic, striking the side of the archway where it had been weakened. A brick fell out. A crack appeared.

Father Damico leaped and pulled boy and animal out of the way as, with a roar, the side of the arch collapsed, laying bare a piece of the old wall and the hollow behind it before everything vanished in a cloud of dust.

But when the dust settled, the Bishop, his eyes starting from his head, was pointing to something that rested in a niche of the hollow just revealed. It was a small, grey, leaden box. Even from there they could see the year 1226, when St Francis died, engraved on the side, and the large initial 'F'.

The Bishop's breath came out like a sigh. 'Ah, could it be? The legacy of St Francis! Fra Leo mentions it. It was hidden away centuries ago, and no one has ever been able to find it since.'

The Supervisor said hoarsely, 'The contents! Let us see what is inside – it may be valuable!'

The Bishop hesitated. 'Perhaps we had best wait. For this is in itself a miracle, this finding.'

But Father Damico, who was a poet and to whom St Francis was a living spirit, cried, 'Open it, I beg of you! All who are here are humble. Surely Heaven's plan has guided us to it.'

The Abbot held the lantern. The mason with his careful, honest workman's hands deftly loosed the bindings and pried the lid off the airtight box. It opened with an ancient creaking of its hinge and revealed what had been placed there more than seven centuries before.

There was a piece of hempen cord, knotted as though, perhaps, once it had been worn about the waist. Caught in the knot, as fresh as though it had grown but yesterday, was a single sprig of wheat. Dried and preserved, there lay, too, the stem and starry flower of a mountain primrose and, next to it, one downy feather from a tiny meadow bird.

Silently the men stared at these objects from the past to try to read their meaning, and Father Damico wept, for to him they brought the vivid figure of the Saint, half-blinded, worn and fragile, the cord knotted at his waist, singing, striding through a field of wheat. The flower might have been the first discovered by him after a winter's snow, and addressed as 'Sister Cowslip', and praised for her tenderness and beauty. As though he were transported there, Father Damico saw the little field bird fly trustingly to Francis' shoulder and chirrup and nestle there and leave a feather in his hand. His heart was so full he thought he could not bear it.

The Bishop, too, was close to tears as, in his own way, he interpreted what they had found. 'Ah, what could be clearer than the message of the Saint? Poverty, love, and faith. This is his bequest to all of us.'

Pepino said, 'Please, lords and sirs, may Violetta and I go into the crypt now?'

They had forgotten him. Now they started up from their contemplation of the touching relics.

Father Damico cleared the tears from his eyes. The doorway was freed now, and there was room for boy and donkey to pass. 'Ah, yes,' he said. 'Yes, Pepino. You may enter now. And may God go with you.'

The hoofs of the donkey went sharply *clip-clop, clip-clop* on the ancient flagging of the passageway. Pepino did not support her now, but walked beside, hand just resting lightly and lovingly on her neck. His round, cropped head with the outstanding ears was held high, and his shoulders were bravely squared.

And to Father Damico it seemed, as they passed, whether because of the uneven light and the dancing

shadows, or because he wished it so, that the ghost, the
merest wisp, the barest suspicion of a smile had returned
to the mouth of Violetta.

Thus the watchers saw boy and donkey silhouetted
against the flickering oil lamps and altar candles of the
crypt as they went forward to complete their pilgrimage
of faith.

LOVE OF SEVEN DOLLS

To Burr Tillstrom and Fran Allison

PART ONE

IN PARIS, IN THE SPRING of our times, a young girl was about to throw herself into the Seine.

She was a thin, awkward creature with a wide mouth and short black hair. Her body was all bones and hollows where there should have been curves and flesh. Her face was appealing, but it was now gaunt with hunger and the misery of failure. Her eyes were haunting, large, liquid, dark and filled with despair.

Her name was Marelle Guizec, but her nickname was Mouche. She was an orphan, a Bretonnaise from the village of Plouharg, near St Brieuc. Wretched though she was, some of the mystery of this mysterious land still clung to her. It manifested itself in the grace with which she walked as though still clad in the swinging peasant skirts, the gravity of her glance, her innocence and primitive mind in which for all her youth — she was only twenty-two — were dark corners of Celtic brooding. One of these was now leading her to her death.

She wished to die, for like many young girls from the provinces she had come to Paris to try to succeed in the theatre. She had failed most miserably. There was truly no single soul in the world who cared what became of her now that she had been dismissed from the lowly *Moulin Bleu Revue* as incompetent and incapable of inspiring interest or desire amongst the patrons. There was no one who was her friend. The paltry francs she would receive would feed and shelter her for only a few days. After that she must starve or sell herself.

Do you remember Paris that May when spring came early and the giant candelabra of the chestnut trees in bloom illuminated the beautiful city?

The sun-washed days were warm, but the nights still cold and often windy. By day Paris played at summer; the children appeared with their nurses by the Rond Point, the scent of perfumed women lingered on the boulevards, the gay shops glittered in the sunlight; the sky was a canopy of that particular blue that seems to exist only over France. But in the evening, the chill drove people off the streets.

It was for this reason that the early season street carnival beyond the Pont Neuilly was preparing to pack up and depart in disappointment, for it had expected to do most of its business after dark.

Its chain of nakedly glaring electric-light bulbs and smoking gasolene flares stretched along one side of the Avenue General de Gaulle from the Rond Point de la Defence all the way to the bridge across the Seine that gave entrance to Paris from the west.

The clangour of the street fair, the carousel music, the cries of the barkers and snapping of rifles in the shooting galleries, the ringing of bells and snorting of the engines that operated the rides had given way to the more prosaic sounds of dismantling, hammering and sawing, and the noise of boards and metal sheets being thrown to the ground and flats being loaded on trucks was drowning out the last of the mechanical music-makers.

Only a few hardy stragglers defied the chill breeze and hung about as swings, whip rides, auto dodgems, stages and tents began to come down. By morning, nothing but the litter in the street and the worn patches on the earth at the side of the broad avenue would indicate where the fair had been.

In the draughty, outdoor canvas-enclosed square that served the shivering girls of the tawdry *Moulin Bleu Revue* as a dressing-room Mouche, having surrendered the scanty bits of costume that had been lent her, donned her clothes and reflected for the last time upon the collapse of her hopes.

The cheap grind and strip show was packing to move on to St Germaine, but she had not been good enough even to keep this job and go along. At the conclusion of the final performance that night the manager had discharged her, saying, 'Too thin, too thin, my child. Our girls run more to meat and juice. I heard someone in the audience say of you, "Here comes that little plucked chicken again." Sorry, but you won't do. If a girl cannot sing or dance, at least she must look like something.'

It was true. Mouche excited pity rather than desire.

Her story was the usual one of the stage-struck girl encouraged by perhaps a local success at some amateur theatricals. Orphaned during the war, she had lived with a great-aunt, who had likewise died when she was but sixteen. She had then gone to St Brieuc and secured a job cleaning the town hall, saving her money until she had sufficient to make the journey to Paris.

And there she had come face to face with the fact that she had neither the talent nor the physical equipment to further her ambitions.

She had been pawed by dirty men and stripped by agents and managers, who had examined the merchandise of her body and in the end had laughed and turned her out undamaged, for her innocence and chastity was an affront to their consciences and they wished to have her out of their sight.

Occasionally she had succeeded in securing a trial in the cabarets of Pigalle and Montmartre and this had kept her from starvation, but she never was able to hold a job, and, descending always lower, had ended with the strip revue in the street fair and now had been judged unfit for this most miserable of forms of entertainment. Not even to the tawdry audiences that filed through the tents for a few francs could her body deliver a single, solitary illusion.

It was this that determined her to do away with herself, for the dismissal pointed up the fact that even had she come to the point of selling herself to keep from starvation she would have found no buyers.

Mouche looked about her once more at the chattering girls who at least were useful in that they could walk across a plank stage and make men shout, or laugh and whistle. Then she collected her few belongings and packed them into the small straw valise she had brought with her, as she had expected to be travelling with them in the bus to their next stop.

She would have no further need for these articles, but she could not bring herself to abandon them. The straw suitcase would be found standing on the parapet of the Pont Neuilly in the morning when the police came with their long poles and fished her body out of the Seine.

She picked up the bag and without a backward glance went out of the enclosure. It seemed as if in anticipation of her rendezvous the light was already extinguished from her eyes. Her thin shoulders had the droop of the beaten girl so easily recognised in France, the soon-to-be suicide . . .

The manager emerged just then and recognising it, was, for a moment, moved to pity and tempted to reverse his decision and call her back. But he hesitated. If one had pity on every little scarecrow from the provinces, where would one end?

And yet there was something appealing about the little one. He had felt it. Not what the customers wanted, but still – if one could catch what it was . . . By the time he had decided to yield to his better nature and called after her, 'Allo! Mouche! Wait. Come back. Perhaps . . .' she was gone.

Mouche, marching unseeing, like one already dead, towards the Seine, thought briefly of her childhood in Brittany and saw again the blue-green seas crashing in white foam onto the black rocks, the sunny fields cut by crooked stone walls and the flames of the poppies from the midst of which rose the ancient stone crosses and still more ancient Druid menhirs.

The fisherboats beat their way home; children played in the sand; the postman on his bicycle rode by; women stopped for a gossip outside the baker's cottage and for a moment Mouche smelled the fresh bread and crisp rolls. She was in church again and heard the rustle of starched head-dresses and the sigh of the organ. Snatches of melodies of old songs drifted through her mind and for an instant she saw her mother's work-worn hands arranging her first Communion dress. Recollections came to her of old friends, a grey rabbit she had once owned and a tortoise, a yellow cat and a duck that had only one leg. She remembered the eyes of wild things that sometimes peered from the depth of hedges in not unfriendly fashion.

Looking into this bright garden of life as through a

door opened in a wall, yet she could not see how much there was to live for, that she was young and that one could build anew upon the ashes of failure. The black, smoky night, so noisy, cold and hostile, encouraged only the sunless corners of her mind. She hurried forward as one who goes unseeing.

Something, or someone cried out of the darkness: 'Hello there, you with the suitcase! Where are you going and what's your hurry?'

Mouche paused, startled and bewildered, for the shrill little voice obviously was directed at her, but she could not make out whence it came. The impudence of the query angered her for it had the effect of returning her to a world she had in effect already departed.

The next words reaching her out of the darkness startled her even more.

'It's cold at the bottom of the river, little one, and the eels and the crayfish eat your flesh.'

This was magic and Mouche had all the superstition and belief in the supernatural of the Bretonnaise. Fearfully she gazed about her for the source of the voice that could guess her secret.

By the wavering light of a gasolene flare she saw only an empty puppet booth with an oilcloth sign across the top announcing, 'CAPITAINE COQ ET SA FAMILLE.' Nearby, on one side, a dirty-looking gypsy fortune-teller was quarrelling with her husband over the small pickings while they occupied themselves with dismantling their tent. On the other, two men were engaged in loading a strength-testing machine onto a small truck. No one appeared to be aware of the presence of the girl.

The insistent piping voice attacked her again: 'What's the big tragedy? Your boyfriend give you the air? There's plenty more fish in the sea.'

Peering through the smoky haze Mouche now saw that the puppet booth was not entirely deserted as she had first thought. A doll was perched on the counter, or at any rate, half a doll, for no legs were visible, a boy with red hair, bulb nose and pointed ears. He was regarding her with impertinent, painted eyes and a curiously troubled expression on his countenance. In the shifting yellow flicker of the gasolene flare he seemed to be beckoning to her.

'Well?' he said. 'Cat got your tongue? Speak up when you're spoken to.'

In her first alarm, Mouche had set down her valise. Now she picked it up and walked with it slowly closer to the booth to examine this astonishing little creature.

Still feeling strangely indignant at being thus unceremoniously accosted she heard herself to her surprise reply: 'Really, what makes you think it is any of your concern?'

The puppet looked her carefully up and down. 'Oh,' he said. 'Out of a job, down at the heels and huffy too. I was only trying to be polite and pass the time.'

[68]

'By speaking to strangers to whom you have not been introduced?' Mouche chided. 'And getting personal too. How would you like it if I . . .?' She paused, realising for the first time that she was addressing the little creature as though it were a human being. And yet it was not really strange that she should, for its attitudes and movements were so real and even the expression on the painted face seemed to change with the angle of the head.

'Oh, I wouldn't mind,' he concluded for her. 'Every one likes to talk about themselves. Would you care to hear my life story? I was born in a tree on Christmas Eve . . .'

There was a swift movement and a girl puppet appeared on the counter. She had golden ringlets, wide, staring eyes and a small, discontented mouth.

She turned this way and that, appearing to inspect Mouche from all angles. Then she said, 'My goodness, Carrot Top, where do you find them?'

The leprechaun puppet took a bow and said, 'Not bad, eh?'

The girl gave a little shriek. 'My goodness, Carrots, you surely don't think *she's* pretty . . . Why, she's nothing but skin and bones.'

Carrot Top with a twist of his head managed to look reflective. 'Well, I'll admit her legs aren't much to look at, Gigi, but she has nice eyes and there's something about her that . . .'

[69]

'Country trash, if you ask me, and probably no better than she should be,' Gigi murmured and, folding her hands piously, gazed skywards.

'Yes,' Carrot Top agreed. 'A country cousin all right. But still you know . . .'

Mouche felt that it was enough. She stamped her foot at the mocking little creatures and cried, 'Really! How dare you two stand there and discuss me . . . Don't you know that is the worst manners?'

Carrot Top seemed taken aback and looked worried. He replied, 'Dear me. Perhaps you are right. We've all been running somewhat wild of late. Maybe what we need is a little discipline. Why don't you try saying something rude to us?'

Gigi flounced petulantly. 'Well, I for one don't intend to remain here to be abused by a scarecrow,' and vanished beneath the counter.

Carrot Top looked after her and shook his head slowly. 'She's not getting any better-tempered. Well, go ahead. I don't mind being insulted.'

Mouche could not repress a smile. 'I can't. I think I like you.'

'Oh! Do you really?' Carrot Top contrived to look both pleased and startled. 'That wants some thinking over. I'll see you later maybe.'

He vanished likewise but was immediately replaced by the fore part of a red fox with a long, pointed nose and a sardonic grin. There was a leer in his avid eyes and a worse one in his voice. For a moment he watched the girl warily, then appearing to smile a sly, oily smile, rasped at Mouche, 'Hello, baby!'

Mouche gave him a severe look. 'Don't you hello *me*,' she admonished. 'You're a wicked scoundrel if ever I saw one.'

The fox turned his head on his neck so that he looked hurt. 'I am not. I can't help my looks. Come on over here and see. Put your hand out.'

Mouche moved closer to the booth and extended her hand gingerly. The expression on the pale brow beneath her cheap little hat was half worried, yet she felt herself charmed. The fox gently snuggled his chin onto Mouche's palm and heaved a deep sigh. 'There,' he said, 'you see how you've misjudged me?' He cocked an eye up at her.

Mouche was not to be deceived. She remarked, 'I'm not sure I have at all.'

'Heart like a kitten,' the fox insisted, snuggling his chin deeper into the cup of Mouche's palm, and then added, 'The trouble is, nobody trusts me. You would trust me, wouldn't you?'

She was about to reply that she wouldn't dream of doing so, when he moved his head and looked up at her once more. His mouth opened and closed silently. Surely it was the smoky light and the dancing shadows, but Mouche thought she saw such an expression of yearning, such a desire for trust on the sharp, clever face that she

[71]

felt herself unaccountably touched and cried from her own heart, 'Oh yes. I would . . .'

She had all but forgotten whither she had been bound, or why.

Nor did it strike her as at all strange that she should be standing there by the counter of a puppet booth conversing with a scallywag of a fox. Where she came from, one talked not only with the little animals of the fields and the birds in the trees, but the trees themselves and the running brooks, and often one whispered one's innermost secrets or heart's desire to one of the grey dolmens that stood so mysteriously in a meadow.

The fox sighed again. 'I knew I'd find someone innocent enough some day. What's your name, baby?'

'Marelle. But they call me Petite Mouche.'

'Little fly, eh? My name is Mr Reynardo, J.L. Reynardo — Rey to my friends. Where are you from?'

'Plouharg, near St Brieuc.'

The fox suddenly raised his head so that he was looking at her sidelong out of one wicked eye. He quoted from an old proverb, 'Beware a sleeping dog, a praying drunk or a Bretonnaise.'

Mouche snatched her hand away and quoted back at him: 'When the fox preaches, guard your geese . . .'

Mr Reynardo let out a yapping bark of laughter and retired to the side of the booth. 'Kid, you've got some guts in that skinny carcass of yours. Hasn't she, friends?'

This last was addressed to the workmen who had

finished loading the lorry and were now standing by listening.

'She had your measure, old boy,' one of them replied, grinning.

The fox yapped again and then called down below the counter, 'Hey, Ali! Come up here a moment and see if you can scare this one.'

The upper portion of a huge, tousle-headed, hideous, yet pathetic-looking giant rose slowly from beneath and stared fixedly at Mouche, who stared back. She could not help herself.

Mr Reynardo performed the introductions: 'This is our giant, Alifanfaron – Ali for short. Ali, this is Mouche and she's crazy about me.'

Mouche started to reply indignantly, 'I am not,' but thought better of it and decided to let it go and see what would happen. The giant seemed to be trying desperately to recall something and finally said in a mild, friendly voice, 'Fi-fo-fe . . . No no – fo-fe-fi – Oh dear. That isn't it either. I never seem to get it straight.'

Mouche prompted him, 'Fe-fi-fo . . .'

Ali nodded his head. 'Of course. And then the last one is *fum*. But what's the use? I don't really frighten you, do I?'

On an odd impulse, Mouche solemnly felt her heart beat for a moment and then replied, 'Oh, I'm so sorry. I'm afraid you don't.'

The giant said sadly, 'Never mind. I'd really rather be

[73]

friends. Then I can have my head scratched. Please scratch my head.'

Obediently, Mouche gently rubbed the wooden head while Ali sighed and pushed slightly against her fingers like a cat. Once more Mouche felt herself strangely moved and even more so when the fox yipped, 'Me too, me too,' like a child that has been left out of something, and came whipping over and leaned his head against her shoulder.

A battered and paint-shy old Citroën with a luggage rack on the roof and a trunk fastened to the rear drove alongside the booth from out of the darkness, and a fearful and astonishing apparition climbed out.

He was a one-eyed negro in the tattered remnants of the uniform of a Senegalese line regiment, a wrinkled old man with a large, rubbery face, naked, glistening skull and a mouth full of gold teeth that testified he might once have known more opulent times.

He wore not a black, but a soiled white patch over his blind left eye which gave him a terrifying aspect though this was belied, however, by an innocent and child-like grin. There were sergeant's stripes on the uniform sleeve and he had an old World War I *kepi* on the back of his head. Around his neck was slung a guitar.

He took in the group and shook his head in marvel, chuckling, 'Whooeeeee! Who you chasing up this time, Mr Reynardo? Can't leave you alone two minutes before you go making eyes at something in skirts.'

Mr Reynardo leered at the Senegalese. 'You, Golo! Cough up that ten franc piece I saw you palm when you took up that last collection this evening.'

The Senegalese grinned admiringly. 'You saw that, Mr Reynardo? By my life, you don't miss much, do you?' He fished the coin out of his pocket and laid it down on the counter where the fox immediately pounced on it, saying to Mouche virtuously, 'You see? It's good someone is honest around here. Golo, this is a friend of mine, by the name of Mouche. We're thinking of getting married. Mouche, meet Golo. He's our orchestra.'

Mouche found herself shaking hands solemnly with the negro who bowed courteously and carried her hand half way to his lips as though she were a queen.

Mr Reynardo rasped, 'Break it up. You'll be giving her ideas.' Then to Mouche, 'By the way, kid, can you sing?'

Mouche replied, 'A little. Can you?'

'Oh yes,' Mr Reynardo admitted. 'Heroic tenor. And I've got a friend who is a pretty good basso. We could have a trio. Hey, Ali, send the Doc up. Golo, you play something for us.'

The giant disappeared to be replaced by a solemn-looking penguin who wore a pince-nez attached to a black ribbon and was introduced by the fox as Dr Duclos, a member of the academy.

The penguin bowed and murmured, 'Charmed indeed. Forgive the formal clothes. I have just come from the annual dinner of the Anthropofumbling Society.'

Golo leaned against the dented wing of the Citroën and fingered the advance ghost of a melody on his guitar, then struck a firm chord and thereafter, without further introduction, Mouche found herself singing the popular Parisian song hit of the moment:

> 'Va t'en, va t'en, va t'en!
> Je ne suis plus ton amant . . .'

She had not much voice, it was true, but there was a softness and an ingenuous earnestness in it with a slight throaty quality that was young and pleasing and blended astonishingly well with the unctuous but not unmelodious tenor sung by Mr Reynardo, supported and interlarded by deep basso 'poom-pooms' contributed at the proper musical moments by Dr Duclos.

> 'Be off, be off, be off!
> I am not your lover any more . . .
> Another has taken your place . . .'

The music completed the spell under which Mouche found herself and carried her away into this strangest of all strange lands of make-believe into which she had wandered out of the unhappy night.

The song was catching the ears of their neighbours too. The fortune teller and her husband ceased quarrelling and came nearer to listen, their gypsy eyes glistening

[76]

in the torchlight. The workman and the truck driver were clapping their hands to punctuate the *'Va t'en'*. A passing cab-driver pulled up to the kerb and got out. Late home-goers lingered. Other concessionaires came over from nearby pitches which they had been engaged in dismantling. Soon a considerable crowd had formed a semi-circle about the dingy little puppet booth.

These were hard, rough people, mostly; the night was cold and the hour late, but they too succumbed to the spell of the odd little talking dolls, the music and the new ingredient that had been added – the waif.

Even this brief space of time had seen a transformation worked in Mouche. The listlessness and despair had been shed. If anything, her gauntness, the hunger-thin frame and the large, tender, believing eyes shining from the pale countenance added to the attraction as in company with the sly-looking, amorous fox and the pompous, stuffy, over-dignified penguin she acted out the verses of the song, playing first to one and then the other as though she had really changed lovers.

They ended with a shout and a thump of Golo's guitar and his hearty chuckle was heard above the applause and bravos of the audience. Mouche did not even notice Golo reach behind the booth for a battered tin *poilu's* helmet with which he passed swiftly through the crowd, or the response to his collection in bills and coins, for she was too absorbed with Mr Reynardo and Dr Duclos who were taking elaborate bows.

[77]

'You were in excellent voice tonight, my dear Reynardo.'

'Permit me to compliment you likewise, friend Duclos.'

To Mouche, Reynardo remarked, 'You know, I could make something out of you, Baby . . .' and Dr Duclos added importantly, 'Your *sol-fege* is not at all bad, my child. I say of course that everything is diaphragm control . . .'

From somewhere in the depths of the booth a bell rang. Mr Reynardo let out a yelp. 'Oops! Supper! Sorry. Nice to have met you, kid. Come on, Doc.'

The fox and the penguin disappeared beneath the stage. Golo regarded Mouche for a moment with the sad creamy eyes of an old negro who had seen much. He said, 'Who are you, Miss?'

Mouche replied, 'Nobody.'

'You brought us good luck.'

'Did I? I'm glad.'

'Where you go now?'

'I don't know.'

His question had restored the chill to the night and the feel of the hard-packed earth beneath her feet. The fairy tale was over then. Yet the echoes still lingered and her heart felt strangely light.

Golo nodded. To have no place to go was familiar to him. He said, 'You excuse me, Miss. I better get things ready to move.'

[78]

He went to the car and unstrapped the big theatrical trunk from the rear. Someone at Mouche's elbow went 'Pssst!' Another half-doll occupied the stage, an elderly woman with a pronounced moustache and indignant eyebrows. She was wearing a coverall and mob cap and carried a dustcloth with which she took an occasional wipe at the counter. When Mouche turned to her she first peered furtively to both sides and then addressed her in a hoarse whisper.

'Don't trust them.' Instantly Mouche was swept back to this other world. 'Don't trust whom?' she asked.

'Don't trust *anyone*. I am a woman, and believe me, I know what I am talking about.'

'But they were all so kind . . .' Mouche protested.

'Hah! That's just how they do it. I am Madame Muscat, the concierge here. I know everything that goes on. You look as though you might be a respectable girl. The things I could tell you . . . They're all a bad lot and if you take my advice you won't have anything to do with them.'

Mouche was not one to listen to gossip and Madame Muscat was exactly like all the concierges she had ever known. Nevertheless she felt a pang at her heart, the kind one experiences when ill is spoken of dear friends. She cried, 'Oh surely that can't be so . . .'

Golo went by carrying the trunk on his shoulders. He paused and said reprovingly: 'You oughtn't to say things like that, Madame Muscat. They ain't really so bad. They just young and a little wild.' To Mouche he said reassuringly, 'Don't you pay her any attention, Miss. Wait until I put her in this trunk again. That will keep her quiet.'

Madame Muscat gave a little shriek at the threat and ducked quickly beneath the counter as Golo continued on behind the booth.

In her place there appeared then finally one more puppet, an old gentleman who wore square steel-rimmed spectacles, a stocking cap and leather apron. The expression painted on his face contrived sometimes to be quizzical and friendly, at others, when he moved his head, searching and benign. For a moment he appeared to look right through Mouche. Then in a gentle voice he spoke to her saying, 'Good evening to you. My name is Monsieur Nicholas. I am a maker and mender of toys. My child, I can see you are in trouble. Behind your eyes are many more tears than you have shed.'

Mouche's hand flew to her throat because of the ache that had come to lodge there. It had been so long since anyone had called her 'child'.

Monsieur Nicholas said, 'Perhaps you could care to tell me about it.'

Golo appeared again. He said, 'You tell *him*, Miss. He is a good man. Everybody who has troubles tells them to Monsieur Nicholas.'

Now the tears came swiftly to Mouche's eyes and with their flow something loosened inside her so that

standing there in the garish light before the shabby
puppet booth and the single animated wooden doll
listening so attentively to her, the story of her trials and
failures poured from her in moving innocence, for she
could not have confessed it thus to any human.

When she had reached the end of her unhappy
tale, Monsieur Nicholas concluded for her, '. . . And
so you were going to throw yourself into the Seine
tonight.'

Mouche stared, marvelling. 'How did you know?'

'It was not hard to tell. There is nothing to seek for
one as young as you at the bottom of the river.'

'But, Monsieur Nicholas – what shall I do? Where
shall I go?'

The puppet bowed his head as he reflected gravely
for a moment, a tiny hand held to his brow. Then he
tilted his head to one side and asked, 'Would you care to
come with us?'

'Come with you? Oh, could I? Do you suppose I
could?' It was as though suddenly a vista of Heaven had
opened for Mouche. For she loved them already, all of
these queer, compelling little individuals who each in a
few brief moments had captured her imagination or
tugged at her heartstrings. To make-believe for ever – or
as the day was long, to escape from reality into this
unique world of fantasy . . . She held out her arms in
supplication and cried, 'Oh, Monsieur Nicholas! Would
you really take me with you?'

[81]

The puppet contemplated silently for a moment and then said, 'You must ask Poil du Carot. Officially, he manages the show. Goodbye.'

The stage remained empty for an appreciable time. Then an insouciant whistling was heard and Poil du Carot appeared bouncing jauntily along the counter, looking nowhere in particular. As though surprised he said, 'Oh, hello, Mouche, you still here?'

The girl was uncertain how to approach him. He was mercurial. His mood now seemed to be quite different. She ventured: 'Monsieur Nicholas said . . .'

Carrot Top nodded. 'Oh yes. I heard about it.'

'May I come please, dear Carrot Top?'

The doll with the worried expression looked her over. 'When you ask so prettily it is hard to refuse . . . After all, it was I who discovered you, wasn't it? However, if you come with us you wouldn't always be telling me what to do, would you? You know I have a lot of responsibility with this show.'

'Oh no . . .'

'But you'd look after us, wouldn't you?'

'If you'd let me . . .'

'Sew on buttons and things?'

'Darn socks . . .'

'We have no feet,' Carrot Top said severely. 'That's the first thing you'll have to learn.'

'Then I'd knit you mittens.'

Carrot Top nodded. 'That would be nice. We've

never had mittens. There'd be no money, you know . . .'

'Oh Carrot Top!'

'Mouche!'

Mouche never knew exactly how it happened, but suddenly she was close to the booth, weeping with joy, and Carrot Top had both his arms around her neck and was patting her cheek with one of his little wooden hands. He wailed, 'Mouche, don't cry. I always meant you to come. I only had to pretend because I'm the manager . . . Welcome to Poil du Carot and the family of Capitaine Coq.'

From below there sounded the sardonic yapping of the fox and the shrill voice of Gigi, 'Why does she have to come with us? There isn't enough for everybody now.' Madame Muscat whisked across the stage once croaking, 'Remember, I warned you.' Ali arose and rumbled: 'Gee, I'm glad. I need looking after because I'm so stupid. Scratch my head . . .'

Carrot Top suddenly became efficient. 'Not now, Ali. We've got to get cracking. Golo . . . Golo, where are you?'

'Right here, little boss.' The Senegalese appeared from behind the booth.

'Mouche is coming with us. Find her a place in the car . . .'

The negro shouted, 'Bravo. That's mighty good luck for us. I find her a place in the car.'

'Then come back and strike the set, Golo.'

'Yes, sir, little boss. Strike the set. I'll do that. You come along with me, Miss, and I fix you right up.' He picked up Mouche's valise and went with her to the Citroën where he stowed it in the luggage boot in the rear. Then he looked into the back seat of the car which was buried beneath pieces of old clothing, newspapers, maps, bits of costumes for the puppets and props, packages, a bottle of beer, a half-eaten loaf of bread, tools and a spare tin of petrol along with other masculine litter.

Golo began a futile rummaging. 'Don't look like they's much room, but . . .'

Mouche took over. 'Never mind, Golo. I promised Carrot Top I'd look after things. I'll have it tidied up in no time.'

As she worked Mouche sang, '*Va t'en, va t'en, va t'en* . . .' humming the melody happily to herself. But through her head were running new words to the old song, 'Go away, death! You are not my lover any longer. I have found a new one called life. It is to him I shall always be faithful . . .'

She cleared a small space for herself on the seat, folded the clothing and the maps, wrapped the bread and a piece of sausage she found, stowed the costumes carefully where they would not get dirty, and while she was at it, gave a good brushing and cleaning to the old car which in a sense was to be her future home, one that she would share with Carrot Top, Reynardo, Ali, Madame Muscat and Gigi, Golo and all the rest.

So bemused and enchanted was she that not once did she give a thought to that other who would also be there, the unseen puppeteer who animated the seven dolls.

When she had finished it was only the spare tin of petrol which had defeated her and she emerged from the car searching for Golo to ask his advice.

Yet when Mouche discovered him nearby she found herself unable to call, or even speak, so strange and ominous was the sight that met her eyes.

For the booth with all its endearing occupants had vanished from the spot it had occupied and now lay flat, a compact pile of board, canvas, oil-cloth and painted papier mâché, tarpaulined and roped by Golo who was finishing the job with the sure movements of long practice. None of the puppets were in sight and reposed presumably in the trunk that stood nearby.

But the pole with the flaming gasolene torch was still there and against it leaned a man Mouche had not seen before. He was clad in corduroy trousers, rough shoes and was wearing a roll-neck sweater under some kind of old army fatigue-jacket. A stocking cap was pulled down on one side of his head and a cigarette hung from his lips.

In the wavering light it was not possible to judge his age, but his attitude and the expression on his face and mouth was cold, cynical and mocking. His eyes were

fixed on Mouche and she could see their glitter
reflecting the torchlight.

It was like a chill hand laid upon her heart, for there
was no warmth or kindliness in the figure lounging
against the pole, his fists pressed deeply into the pockets
of his jacket. The shine of his eyes was hostile and the
droop of the cigarette from his lips contemptuous.

Mouche, in her marrow, knew that this was the
puppet-master, the man who had animated the little
creatures that had laid such an enchantment upon her,
yet she was filled with dread. For a moment even she
hoped that somehow this was not he, the master of the
dolls, but some other, a pitch-man, a labourer, or
lounger from a neighbouring concession.

Golo, straightening up from his task, looked from one
to the other, the silent man, the frightened girl, and
presented them to one another elaborately, as though
they had never met before, as though the man had not
been able to look through the one-way curtain behind
which he sat as he gave life and voice to his puppets, and
study each curve and hollow of the girl's face, and every
line of her thin body.

'Miss Mouche, this is Capitaine Coq,' Golo explained
and then turned to the man who had not stirred.
'Capitaine, this here is Miss Mouche. Carrot Top, he find
her walking along in the dark by herself, crying, and he
stop her and have a talk with her. Then Mr Reynardo he
find out she a pretty damn good singer, and Monsieur

Nicholas he come up and ask maybe she like to come along with us, after that old gossip Madame Muscat she try to make trouble. Then Carrot Top he say okay she can come along with the show. I think that very good luck for everybody.' He paused, satisfied. Golo was convinced that the little creatures thought and acted as individuals and that the puppeteer was not privy to what they said and did, or what transpired between them.

Mouche, too, had been under the same spell, and the presence of the man confused and alarmed her and increased the turmoil of her emotions.

The man introduced as Capitaine Coq moved his eyes slightly so as to take in Golo and rasped, 'Well, what do you expect me to do about it? What did Carrot Top tell you to do?'

'To get the gear on the car, Monsieur le Capitaine . . .'

'Well then, get on with it. And you drive. I want to get some sleep.'

'Get the gear onto the car. Okay, sir . . .' Golo picked up the heavy bundle, but was slow in moving. The Capitaine barked, 'Allez!' at him and helped him with a kick.

Golo did not exclaim or protest. Mouche thought she would die of shame and sadness because of the manner in which the negro scuttled under the impetus of the blow, like an animal – or a human who has well learned the futility of protest against cruelty.

Reality as cold as the night engulfed Mouche. The man's personality and harshness was as acrid as the stench from the smoking flare above his head. Now he turned his calculating stare upon Mouche and for the first time spoke directly to her. He did not remove the cigarette from his lips and it hung there remaining horrifyingly motionless when he talked, for he had the professional ventriloquist's trick of speaking without moving his lips, when he wished.

'You, Mouche! Come here.'

She felt herself hypnotised. She was unable to resist moving slowly towards him. When she stood in front of him he looked her up and down.

'You needn't waste any sympathy on Golo,' he said, again having read her. 'He has a better life than he would have elsewhere. Now you listen to me . . .' He paused and the cigarette end glowed momentarily. Mouche felt herself trembling. 'You can stay with us as long as you behave yourself and help with the act. If you don't, I'll kick you out, no matter what Carrot Top says. Carrot Top likes you. Rey and Dr Duclos seem to think you can sing. That baby bleat of yours makes me sick, but it pulled in the francs from that crowd tonight and that's all I care. Now get into the back of that car. You may have some bread and sausage if you're hungry. But not a sound out of you. March!'

Had she had her suitcase in her possession, Mouche would have turned and fled. But it was locked now in the luggage boot and she had a woman's inability to part with her possessions no matter how wretched they might be. And besides, where was she to go? Not the river any more, at the bottom of which writhed eels and crayfish as Carrot Top had warned her.

Half-blinded with tears, Mouche turned away and obeyed him.

She heard the scraping and thudding on the roof as Golo fastened the dismantled puppet booth to the rack and then tied the trunk on behind.

Capitaine Coq got into the front seat, pulled his stocking cap over his eyes and went to sleep. The car, guided by Golo, moved off, crossing the bridge and turning north at the Port Neuilly, sought the high road to Rheims.

Huddled in the back seat, Mouche dried her tears and nibbled on the bread and sausage. She managed to derive comfort from the fact that safe in the trunk behind her, tarpaulined against inclement weather, were all the little creatures who had seemed to like her. And she remembered that even Capitaine Coq had spoken of them in the third person as though their lives were their own.

Just before she fell asleep, she felt the trunk scrape against the rear of the car and she smiled, thinking of Poil du Carot, bowed beneath his managerial worries, the hypocritical but lovable fox, the unhappy giant, the sulky golden-haired girl, the pompous but friendly penguin, the gossipy concierge who at bottom was a woman who could be trusted, and the kind and touching mender of broken toys. Surely she would be meeting them all again . . .

Part Two

THE REAL NAME of the man who billed himself as Capitaine Coq was Michel Peyrot, and he was bred out of the gutters of Paris, the same which in an earlier age had spawned Villon.

His had been a life without softness or pity. He had never known his father. When he was six his mother, who earned her living on the streets, was murdered. Michel was taken by a carnival family. His foster-mother, a worn-out soubrette, augmented her income by obliging clients behind the tent after the performance; his foster father was a fire-eater in the freak show and was rarely sober.

When Michel was twelve, the fire-eater engaged in a duel with a rival from another fair, but being drunk, miscalculated the amount of petrol he could store in his cheeks to blow out from his mouth in flames. Swallowing some which became ignited simultaneously he died horribly of internal combustion. His wife, already undermined with disease, did not survive him long, and at thirteen Michel was again alone in the world.

[91]

By the time he was fifteen, he was a little savage
practised in all of the cruel arts and swindles of the street
fairs and cheap carnivals. Now at thirty-five he was
handsome in a rakish way, with wiry, reddish hair, wide-
spaced grey eyes in a pale face and a virile crooked nose
wrinkled still further by a blow that had flattened it
during a brief experiment with pugilism and which, with
a sensuous mouth, gave him something of the look of a
satyr.

Throughout his life no one had ever been kind to him,
or gentle, and he paid back the world in like. Wholly
cynical, he had no regard or respect for man, woman,
child or God. Not at any time he could remember in his
thirty-five years of existence had he ever loved anything
or anyone. He looked upon women as conveniences that
his appetite demanded, and after he had used them,
abandoned them or treated them badly. Why he had
picked up the thin wretched bit of flotsam known as
Mouche he could not have told. Indeed, he would have
insisted that it was not he at all who had added her to his
queer family, but the members of that group themselves,
Carrot Top, Monsieur Reynardo, Madame Muscat and
Monsieur Nicholas, who had made the decision.

For in spite of the fact that it was he who sat behind
the one-way curtain in the booth, animated them and
supplied their seven voices, the puppets frequently acted
strangely and determinedly as individuals over whom he
had no control. Michel never had bothered to reflect

greatly over this phenomenon but had simply accepted it as something that was so and which, far from interfering with the kind of life he was accustomed to living, brought him a curious kind of satisfaction.

Growing up with the people of the carnival acts, Michel had learned juggling, sword-swallowing and leaping on the trampoline, but it was in ventriloquism that he became the most proficient.

The lives of the puppets had begun when Michel Peyrot was a prisoner of the Germans during the war, and in their camps had a kind of post graduate course in all that was base in human nature.

In this evil period of an evil life he first carved and clad the seven puppets, brought them to life for the entertainment of his fellow prisoners and made the discovery that more and more they refused to speak the obscenities and vulgarities that make soldiers laugh, but instead were becoming individuals with lives of their own.

During those times that he sat hidden in the puppet booth, Michel Peyrot was not, but the seven were. Golo, the derelict Senegalese, understood this paradox perfectly. To him it was simply the primitive jungle magic by which his spirit was enabled to leave the body and enter into other objects which then became imbued with his life. But there was yet another manifestation of which Michel Peyrot was unaware, and that was that under the scheme of creation it was not possible for a

[93]

man to be wholly wicked and live a life entirely devoted to evil.

If Carrot Top, Gigi and Ali the giant were restoring to him the childhood of which he had been robbed, or Reynardo, Dr Duclos, Madame Muscat and Monsieur Nicholas the means by which he could escape from himself, Michel was not consciously aware of it. Often he was cynically amused at the things done and the sentiments expressed by his creations, for they were completely foreign to him.

Yet the habit of the puppet booth grew and when the war ended and he returned to France, Michel Peyrot became Capitaine Coq, and with Golo, whom he had found starving in the prison camp, as slave, orchestra and factotum took to the road.

The last night of the fair outside the Port Neuilly in Paris, it had been the experienced and cynical eye of Capitaine Coq that had instantly detected the despairing shoulder slope and the blind, suicide walk of the unhappy girl with the straw valise, but it had been Poil du Carot, the puppet with the red hair and pointed ears who had saved her, for Coq would not have given a fig for a whole troupe of despairing girls marching single file into the Seine. He had looked upon women and death and dead women unmoved. But it amused him to let Carrot Top and the others deal with the girl as they wished.

Nevertheless, once the strange little play had begun and the seven had proceeded independently with their work of capturing her, Coq's sharp showman's instincts had been quick to recognise the value of this trusting child speaking seriously and with complete belief across the booth to the inhabitants thereof. Whoever or whatever she was, she was possessed of that indefinable something that bridges the gap separating audience and performer and touches the heart of the beholder. He had noted her effect upon the hardened crowd of pitchmen, labourers and fellow rascals who had gathered about his booth. If the girl could be taught to work thus spontaneously with his family, standing out in front of the counter, she might become a definite business asset. If not, he could always kick her out or abandon her.

But there was one more quality which had attracted him in her, as he had peered through the scrim of the blind curtain and seen her pinched shoulders, hollow cheeks, dark unhappy eyes and snow-white, blue-veined temples beneath the short-cut black hair, or rather which had exasperated him and roused all of the bitterness and hatred of which he had so great a supply. This was her innocence and essential purity. Capitaine Coq was the mortal enemy of innocence. It was the one trait in human beings, man or woman, boy or girl, that he could not bear. He would, if he could, have corrupted the whole world.

In the back of the car, Mouche had slept the sleep of mental and physical exhaustion. When she awoke, it was morning, and she was alone. All of the panic of the night before returned overwhelmingly and she sprang from the machine looking about her fearfully. But the bright sunlight and the surroundings helped to dissipate some of her fears. The dilapidated vehicle was parked in a tangled area behind booths and concessions of yet another fair. In the background she saw the twin towers of the damaged cathedral of Rheims.

There was a water pump nearby and she went to it and washed her face, the cold water helping to clear her head. When she ventured through the tangle of guy wires and stays supporting a nearby tent she heard suddenly a voice with a familiar rasp, 'Hola, Mouche!'

She edged through to the street on which the fair fronted. It was Mr Reynardo. The booth that she had seen only by torch flare the night before was standing once more. It looked shabby in the morning light. But there was no disputing that Mr Reynardo was a fine figure of an impudent red fox.

He whistled at her, opened his jaws and asked, 'Wash your face, baby?'

'Of course,' Mouche replied and then asked pointedly, 'Did you?'

'No, but don't tell anyone. I think I got away with it.' He whipped below and was replaced by Carrot Top who held a one hundred franc note in his two hands. He said:

'Oh hello, Mouche. Sleep all right?'

'Oh yes, thank you. I think so.' The most delicious

relief pervaded her. Here they were again, her little friends of the night before. How natural it seemed to be standing there talking to them.

Carrot Top piped, 'Go get yourself some bread and cheese for your breakfast,' and handed her the note. 'There's an *Epicerie* just down the street. I've still got a lot to do to get the show ready. And bring back the change.'

As she turned to go, somebody behind her went 'Pssssst!' She looked around and saw Mr Reynardo in a corner of the booth motioning to her with his head. She went to him and he stretched his snout up to her ear and whispered hoarsely, 'There needn't *be* any change.'

Mouche asked, 'What do you mean, Mr Reynardo?'

The fox contrived a wicked leer. 'Call me Rey. Shhh . . . Everybody knows prices are up. Say breakfast cost more and keep the difference. But remember, it was my idea. Fifty-fifty, kid . . .'

Mouche shook her head as earnestly as though she were reproving a child. 'But Rey . . . Really! That isn't honest.'

'Ha, ha!' yipped the fox. 'Maybe not, but it's the only way you'll get any money out of this outfit. Don't say I didn't tip you.'

When Mouche returned from her breakfast and with thirty francs left over, Carrot Top and Gigi the ingenué were holding the stage. The leprechaun was trying to comb her hair, the angle of his head giving a worried and concentrated expression to his face. A half-dozen people were standing about watching.

Carrot Top looked up. 'Oh, back again, Mouche? Had your breakfast?'

Mouche replied politely, 'Yes, thank you. And here's your change.'

Carrot Top nodded absently, took the money, disappeared beneath the counter with it and reappeared almost immediately saying, 'I'm trying to do Gigi's hair. It's full of mares' nests.'

Gigi whined sulkily, 'It is not. He's hurting me.'

'Birds' nests, you mean,' Mouche corrected. 'Here, let me help. Girls know how to do that ever so much better.'

Carrot Top looked severe. 'Men make the best hairdressers . . .' he announced, but surrendered the comb to Mouche who applied herself gently to reducing the snarls in Gigi's golden wig.

Gigi commanded, 'I want braids. I'm tired of all that hair in my eyes. Braid my hair, Mouche.'

'Certainly, Gigi,' Mouche acquiesced. 'And then we'll wind it about your ears in two buns, Bretonne fashion.'

Unselfconsciously as though there were no one else watching, she set about combing and separating the hair into strands and then began to weave the braids, singing as she did so, an ancient Breton hair-braiding song that for centuries mothers had sung to their little daughters to keep them quiet during the ceremony. It went:

'First,
One and three
then
Three and two
then
Two and one,
NOW –
One and two
and
Three and one
and
Two and one . . .'

It had a simple, repetitive, hypnotic melody and Golo appearing from behind the booth with his guitar, fingered the strings softly for a moment and picked it up. Doctor Duclos appeared with some sheet music which he read earnestly through the pince-nez affixed to his beak and contributed basso 'poom-pooms'. Gigi beat time with her hands. In no time there was a fascinated and enchanted crowd, ten deep, gathered about the booth.

When the hair was braided and bunned, Gigi and Dr Duclos went away and Carrot Top taking the empty stage explained the plot of their play. He is in love with Gigi, but the girl is being compelled by her greedy mother, Madame Muscat, to marry wealthy windy old Dr Duclos. Carrot Top's friend Reynardo sends the giant

Alifanfaron to abduct Gigi, but being likewise in the
employ of Dr Duclos, the double-crossing fox arranges
for the giant to steal Madame Muscat while he makes
love to Gigi instead.

Into this plot, without further preparation, Mouche
was drawn by the puppets to explain, guide, mother,
scold, keeping their secrets, sharing others with the
audience, while playing a variety of roles, a maid, Mr
Reynardo's secretary, Dr Duclos' sister, a friend of
Madame Muscat's . . .

She had a quick wit for situations, but above all she
had the ability to forget herself and become wholly
immersed in the goings-on. Because she believed so
completely in the little creatures she had the unique
power of transferring this belief to the audience and
with a look, a laugh, or a single tender passage between
herself and one of the puppets, transporting the
watchers away from the hard-packed earth on which
they stood and into the world of make-believe where the
ordinary rules of life and living did not obtain.

Before the little play was over, all concerned had
changed sides so often, that Monsieur Nicholas had to
appear to untangle them and at the finish, to great
applause, Carrot Top and Gigi, Dr Duclos and Madame
Muscat and Ali and Mouche were paired off, for the
poor giant made such a muddle of things that Mouche
had to take him under her wing and he proceeded to fall
desperately and moon-calf in love with her.

That day the collections made by Golo far surpassed anything Coq and his family had earned heretofore, and the puppeteer took a room in a cheap hotel for himself and a servant's room upstairs for Mouche. Golo was still relegated to sleep in the car and watch over the puppets. He did not mind this for he preferred to be with them.

And that night all three ate a good supper at the inn with red wine, of which Coq drank heavily. The drink did not make him mellower, but on the contrary still more scornful and contemptuous of Mouche.

He ate grossly, ignoring her presence, but once when he felt her large eyes upon him in the uneasy silence that lay over their table like an oasis in the centre of the noisy, smoky bistro, he looked up from his eating and snarled at her, 'What the devil got into you this afternoon when Carrot Top asked you what to do to win Gigi and fly away with him in his helicopter? You stood there frozen and staring like an animal. Why didn't you tell him?'

It was not the reproof, but the sudden shifting of the base of this new and marvellous world into which she had been ushered that disturbed Mouche. It was as though there had been an unwarranted intrusion by an outsider.

'Why,' she exclaimed carefully, 'Carrot Top doesn't want to be told what to do. He made me promise before he let me come along that I was never to interfere with him. And besides,' she concluded after a moment of reflection, 'he doesn't really love Gigi at all, because . . .'

She broke off in alarm for Capitaine Coq was staring at her, his face now flushed dark with rage.

'What makes YOU think you know who Carrot Top loves or doesn't love, you milk-faced little fool?'

For a moment Mouche thought the red-headed man was about to hurl his plate of food in her face . . .

Mouche said, 'I . . . I'm sorry. I really don't know . . . I suppose I just guessed. I won't do it again.'

The fury did not abate from the countenance of Coq, but he did not speak to her again and instead took it out on Golo, shouting at him, 'What are you lingering for, you black monkey? Haven't you stuffed yourself enough? Get away back to the car before everything is pilfered . . .'

They continued to eat and drink in heavy silence again until Mouche gathered the courage to speak to him again. In her simple, gentle way she asked, 'Monsieur le Capitaine, why are you always so angry?'

He laid down his knife and fork and stared long at her out of his cold hard eyes. 'Because you are a fool,' he replied finally, 'and I have no time for fools, particularly women.'

Mouche was not hurt, for she was used to living where men were outspoken. And besides she did not think she was clever, or, since the disasters that had happened to her, even talented any longer. Impulsively she reached over and placed her hand upon his in a sweet conciliatory gesture, saying, 'Dear Capitaine Coq – why cannot you be as kind and patient with me as Carrot Top, Dr Duclos and Mr Reynardo? I am sure they thought I was very stupid at times today, but they never showed it.'

The touch of her gentle fingers seemed to sting Capitaine Coq and he snatched his hand away. 'Because your staring eyes and whining innocence make me sick.'

The attack was so savage that the tears came to Mouche's eyes and she nodded her head silently.

'As for them,' Capitaine Coq continued, draining his glass, 'it is no concern of mine what they do. Get along with them if you know what is good for you, during working hours. And keep out of my way at other times. Understood?'

Mouche nodded again. 'I'll try.'

Yet in spite of the harshness of Capitaine Coq which had the effect only of moving her to a kind of pity for him, for he seemed to be so wretched in his furies, the week of the street fair in Rheims was one of the happiest times Mouche had ever known.

The warmth of her relationship with the seven puppets seemed to grow by leaps and bounds and soon she was familiar with their characteristics, their strengths and weaknesses, the striving and ambitious little Carrot Top with the soaring imagination which

[103]

always wished to brush aside earthbound obstacles, and yet was tied down by the responsibility for all the others and the running of the show; the pompous, long-winded, fatuous Dr Duclos, the prototype of every self-satisfied stuffed shirt, who still in his bumbling way was kind, and the vain, foolish, self-centred ingenué Gigi who of all the little dolls, was not.

Most dependent upon her was Alifanfaron, the giant who frightened no one and was so kind-hearted and slow-witted that everyone took advantage of him. He looked pathetically to Mouche for help and protection and some of the most charming passages took place between the ugly, fearful-looking monster and the young girl who mothered him.

She got on the best with Madame Muscat, for the Madame was a woman who had seen life and buried husbands, understood men and felt that women should stick together for mutual protection. She was always Mouche's ally with advice or an aphorism, or a bit of useful gossip as to what was going on backstage, or below the counter, that mysterious domain where the puppets dwelt.

But if Mouche had had to select a favourite of them all, it would have been Mr Reynardo. He touched her most deeply because he was sly, wicked, not quite honest, knew it and wished and tried, but not too fervently, to be better.

He amused her, too. He baited and teased her and

sometimes worked up little intrigues against her with the others, but when it came right down to it he also seemed to love her the most and feel the deepest need for her affection. Much of his yapping was bravado and the moments when Mouche felt almost unbearably touched and happy were when from time to time cracks appeared in his armour of cynicism and through them she caught glimpses of the small child within wanting to be forgiven and loved.

Though he was her friend and counsellor, Mouche remained a little in awe of Monsieur Nicholas, the mender of toys, for he was a dispenser of impartial justice as well as kindness. His glance through his square spectacles always seemed to penetrate her and reach to her innermost secret thoughts.

Child like, too, but in the primitive fashion backed by the dark lore of his race, was Golo. He was indeed the slave that served the puppets and now that Mouche had become as one of them, hers too. He was versed in the mechanics of the show, yet they meant nothing to him. One moment he could be behind the booth assisting Capitaine Coq in a costume change for one of the puppets, handing him props, or hanging the dolls in proper order, head down so that Coq could thrust his hands into them quickly for those lightning appearances and disappearances of the characters, and the next, out front with Mouche, he looked upon them as living, breathing creatures.

The belief in the separate existence of these little people was even more basic with Mouche for it was a necessity to her and a refuge from the storms of life with which she had been unable to cope.

If fundamentally she must have been aware that it was Coq who animated them, she managed to obliterate the thought. For how could one reconcile the man and his creations? And further she rarely saw Capitaine Coq enter or leave the booth, for he was moody and mysterious in his comings and goings. Sometimes he would sit inside for as long as an hour in the early morning, or even late at night, without giving a sign of his presence there, until suddenly one or more of his puppets would appear onstage.

All orders were given, all business directed through Carrot Top, all rehearsals conducted, new songs learned, plots and bits of business discussed with the puppets until conversing with them became second nature to Mouche and it became almost impossible for her to associate this odd family of such diverse characters with the pale, bitter man who was their creator.

When the week of the fair was at an end in Rheims, they moved on to Sedan for three days and thence to Montmedy and Metz, for that year it was Capitaine Coq's intention to tour north-eastern France and Alsace, until the cold weather drove them south.

One night, without warning, Capitaine Coq emerged from the tap room of the sordid little inn on the outskirts of the city, where they were quartered, half drunk and amorous.

It was late. There were no women about, the regulars having long since paired off or disappeared. He bethought himself then of a piece of property he considered belonged to him, the thin girl asleep upstairs in the narrow bedroom under the eaves.

It was time, he thought, as well, that the little ninny learned something and became a woman. And besides, since they were travelling together, it would be cheaper if henceforth they occupied one room – and perhaps, if she was not a stick, convenient too.

But there was yet another darker purpose that sent him prowling up the stairs that led to the attic chamber. It was the fact that her gentleness, innocence and purity of heart were a perpetual affront to him, the kind of man he was and the life that he led. It had been worming him ever since he had first laid eyes on her. Now he could no longer bear it unless he pulled her down to his level and made her as he was.

He tiptoed to her door, bent and listened for a moment, then, turning the handle swiftly, he whipped inside with the furtive speed of one of his own puppets and closed the door behind him.

When Mouche awoke the next morning, the sunshine was pouring in through the dormer window as if to deny the nightmare that had happened to her. She had thought she would not sleep that night, or ever sleep again. Yet, somehow, oblivion had come, and now the day.

She got out of bed and went to the window which looked onto the rear courtyard in the inn where a dog lolloped, a pig lay in the mud, chickens picked at the ground and ducks and a goose waddled through puddles of dirty water.

They reminded her of her childhood and the farmyards of her village in Brittany and she wondered how she could stand there so calmly contemplating them and the memories they aroused, she who would never be as a child again.

Mouche had neither protested nor resisted Capitaine Coq's act of darkness. Out of the darkness he had come, in darkness taken her and to darkness returned, leaving her bruised, defiled and ashamed.

Startled out of her sleep by his presence, she had recognised him when a shaft of moonlight had fallen across his pale face with the crinkled nose, draining the red from his hair, turning it to purple.

For an instant, her heart had leaped, for she thought that perhaps he loved her, and she would not have denied him.

But there was no love in his eyes or in his heart; no whisper came from his lips and too late she knew what was afoot. It would have been of no use to cry out. Besides, where could she have escaped to, naked, alone, friendless and penniless in a strange inn? He was there before she could make a move, intruding himself into her room, her consciousness, her bed, and then her person.

The brutality of his passion brought her close to a climax of her own, one of seemingly unbearable grief, anguish and pain, and once she murmured his name, 'Michel,' piteously. She thought that surely she would die.

Then he was gone at last, leaving her shamed to death because he had abused her so callously without loving her, weeping miserably with humiliation and hurt because of his cynical contempt for her, the disgusting arrogance and carelessness of his possession of her person. He had not given her a single kindly glance, or caress, or kiss; no word, no gentleness. He had left not a solitary ray of hope to illuminate the despair that engulfed her, that within his strong, imprisoning, goatish body there beat a human heart.

And she was the more shamed because of the instinct that told her that despite the horror and brutality, she had yielded and the act and the moment might make her for ever his.

These were the black memories, her thoughts and fears that morning as she washed and clad the body that was no longer a citadel, and prepared to face what the day would bring.

And yet the miracle occurred again, for that day was

yet like any other, except if anything the troupe was still kinder and more friendly to her.

Carrot Top greeted her with a shrill cry of delight when he arrived at the booth. 'Hey, Mouche! Where you been? Do you know what? There's sausage for breakfast. Golo! Give Mouche her sausage.'

As the Senegalese appeared from behind the booth with garlic country sausage and fresh bread on a paper plate, Mr Reynardo popped up from below with a large piece in his jaws and thrust it at her, saying, 'Here. I saved a piece of mine for you. And you *know* how I love sausage . . .'

Mouche said, 'Oh Rey. Did you really? That was sweet of you . . .'

From below a protesting rumble was heard and as Carrot Top vanished Alifanfaron appeared. 'Say, who stole that piece of sausage I was saving for Mouche?'

Shocked at such affrontery Mouche cried, 'Rey, you *didn't* . . .' But the attitude of guilt of the fox condemned him. She said severely, memory of all her own troubles fading, 'Rey, give it back to Ali at once. There. Now, Ali, you may give it to me.'

The giant presented it. 'It's only because I'm so stupid. Rey said he just wanted to borrow it to see if it was as big as his.'

Mouche took it from him, leaned over and kissed the side of his cheek. 'Poor, dear, Ali,' she said. 'Never you mind. It's better to be trusting than to have no principles at all like some people around here . . .'

Reynardo had the grace to look abashed and flattened himself like a dog at the end of the counter. He said, 'I tried to save you a piece of mine, honestly, I did, Mouche, but it got eaten.'

The girl regarded him ruefully. 'Oh, Rey . . .' she cried, but there was tenderness in her voice as well as reproof. How had it happened so quickly that the iron bands that had clamped about her heart were easing, the sadness that had weighed her down was lifting? The play was on again.

Like a flash, at the first indication that she might be relenting, Reynardo whipped across the stage and with a hang-dog look snuggled his head against her neck and shoulder. Madame Muscat made a brief appearance at the far side of the booth with a small feather duster and dusted the proscenium arch vigorously.

'I warned you, didn't I? You can't trust him for a minute.' But she did not say who was not to be trusted. 'When you've buried as many husbands as I have . . .' she began, and then vanished without concluding. Carrot Top reappeared, clutching a pale blue thousand franc note.

'For you, Mouche,' he said. 'Salary for last week.'

Mouche said, 'Oh Carrot Top, really . . .? But ought you? I mean I never . . .'

'It's all right,' the leprechaun replied. 'We held a

meeting this morning and voted you a share. Dr Duclos presided. His speech from the chair lasted forty-seven minutes . . .'

A crowd began to collect at the sight of a young girl in earnest conversation with a doll — the day's work began . . .

All that summer and into the fall they trouped through eastern France and Alsace, slowly working southwards, moving from town to town, sometimes part of a street fair, carnival or kermess, at others setting up the booth in the market place or square of small villages en route in the country without so much as a by-your-leave from the police or local authorities.

When these officials came demanding permits they found themselves disconcertingly having to deal with Carrot Top, Mr Reynardo, Madame Muscat, or Dr Duclos with Mouche endeavouring to help with the explanations, and usually their charm won the day and they were allowed to remain.

Since, by virtue of Mouche's advent, the lean days were over, there was always a bed in an inn, cheap hotel, or farmhouse with a room to spare and sometimes the luxury even of a bath at night after a day spent in the hot sun. Only now Capitaine Coq no longer bothered to engage two rooms but simply shared one and the bed in it with Mouche.

Thus Mouche, without realising it, was possessed by him both by day and by night.

[112]

The days continued to be an enduring enchantment, the nights an everlasting torment, whether he used her for his pleasure, or turned his back upon her without a word and fell into heavy sleep, leaving her lying there trembling. Sometimes he came to the room in a stupor, barely able to stand after hours of drinking in the tap room. When this happened, Mouche looked after him, undressed him, got him into bed and when he cursed or moaned and tossed during the night she got up to give him water to drink or place a wet cloth upon his head.

Capitaine Coq was drinking to excess because he had impaled himself upon the horns of a strange and insoluble dilemma, and he did not know what to do, except consume wine until all sensation and memory was gone.

On the one hand he was taking all that he wanted or needed from Mouche. She was a growing asset to the show and he was beginning to make money. Further, she was a captive bedmate for whom he need feel no responsibility. But on the other he had made the discovery that while he had indeed been able to ravage her physically, he had never succeeded in destroying her innocence.

He hungered to annihilate it even though at the same time he knew that this was the very quality that drew the audiences and communicated itself to them. Wishing her as soiled and hardened as he was, he debauched her at night and then willy-nilly restored her in the daytime through the medium of the love of the seven dolls, so that phoenix-like she arose each day from the ashes of abuse of the night before, whether it was a tongue lashing, or a beating, or to be used like a woman of the streets. She was rendered each time as soft, and dewy eyed, as innocent and trusting as she had been the night he had first encountered her on the outskirts of Paris.

The more cruelly he treated her, the kindlier and more friendly to her were the puppets the next morning. He seemed to have lost all control over them.

As for Mouche, she lived in a turmoil of alternating despair and entrancing joy.

One night, in Besançon, in a horrible, culminating attempt to break her, Coq appeared in their room with a slut he had picked up in the tavern. They were both drunk.

He switched on the light and stood there looking down at her while she roused herself and sat up. 'Get up and get out,' he commanded.

She did not understand and sat there staring.

'Get out. I'm sick of you.'

She still could not understand what he meant. 'But Michel . . . Where am I to go?'

'To the devil, for all I care. Hurry up and get out. We want that bed . . .'

That night Mouche reached a new depth of shame and humiliation as she dressed beneath the mocking eyes

[114]

of the drab and went out of the room leaving them there. She thought again of dying, but was so confused she no longer knew how to die. For a time she wandered about in a daze through the streets, not knowing where she was going.

Then she came upon the Citroën. Golo was sitting at the wheel smoking a cigarette, his white patch standing out in the light of the street lamp. He appeared to be waiting for her. He got out and took her by the arm.

'You come here and rest, Miss Mouche . . .' he said. He had seen Capitaine Coq go in with the woman and Mouche emerge from the inn, and had followed her. He opened the rear door and she climbed in unseeing and slumped onto the seat. Golo drove to the nearby fairgrounds and parked. The chimes of the musical clock of Besançon announced the hour of three. Mouche began to weep.

Golo reached back and took her small thin hand in his calloused mahogany paw with the fingers hard and scaly from the steel strings of the guitar. But his grip was infinitely tender and his voice even more so as he said, 'Do not cry, my little one . . .' only it sounded even more beautiful and touching in the soft Senegal French, *'Ne pleurez pas, ma petite. Ca fait vous mal aux jolies yeux.'*

Mouche continued to weep as though she would never be able to cease.

Golo got out of the car, was absent for a moment and

then returned. 'Mouche,' he called gently. 'Miss Mouche. You look here. Please Miss Mouche, you look . . .'

The insistence of the soft pleading reached through to Mouche. She took her hands from her face and did as she was bidden. She stared, unbelieving for a moment. Carrot Top and Mr Reynardo were looking at her over the top of the front seat.

'Carrot Top! Rey . . . Oh my darlings . . .' Mouche cried, her heart near to bursting.

The two stared at her woodenly. Between them shone the face of Golo like the mask of an ancient African god carved out of ebony, but an oddly compassionate God. He said sadly, 'They not talk for me, Miss Mouche. But they love you. That's why I brought them here so you remember that. They always love you.'

Mouche reached over and took the two puppets from his hands and cradled the empty husks in her arms and they brought her comfort until her sorely tried spirit rebelled in an outcry that came from her depths, 'But why does he hate me so, Golo, Golo? Why is he so cruel? Why is he so evil?'

The Senegalese reflected before he replied. 'He bewitched. His spirit go out from him. Another come in. Golo see magic like this many years ago in Touba in Senegal when he was a boy.'

Mouche could understand this for she herself came from a country where the supernatural was accepted.

[116]

She said, 'Then you don't hate him, Golo?'

The Senegalese produced another Gaulois and lit it and the match illuminated the cream of his eyeballs. He replied, 'Black man not allowed to hate.'

Mouche drew in her breath sharply. 'Ah,' she cried, 'I hate him! Dear God, how I hate him!'

Golo's cigarette glowed momentarily and he sighed likewise. The noises of the city and the fair were stilled except for the occasional shattering protest of the mangy and hungry lion caged at the far end. He said, 'It good sometimes to hate. But I think it better not to. Sometimes, when you hate, you forget if you sing . . .'

His guitar was by his side and so softly that it was barely audible he plucked out the melody of a Breton lullaby and he hummed it softly. Goodness knows where he had picked it up during the long, rough years of his perpetual exile from the land of his birth, in what camp, prison or country he had heard it sung by another lonely expatriate from the hard-rocked sea-fringed shores of Brittany. He remembered the words after a moment or two:

> 'My young one, my sweeting,
>   Rock in your cradle,
> The sea rocks your father,
>   The sea rocks his cradle,
> God grant you sweet sleep,
>   God grant him return.'

When he played it again, Mouche began to sing it with him, rocking the two dolls in her arms, for that night she was more than half mad from what had been done to her.

Yet Golo had been right; the music worked its magic and the hatred seemed to fade. In its place there returned an echo of that odd compassion she had so often felt for this evil man and which she had never understood.

Golo's eyes were closed and he was singing, dreaming and swaying:

> 'The storm winds are blowing,
>   God rules the storm winds,
> Love God, my sweeting,
>   Safe rides your father,
> God rocks his cradle,
>   God sends you sleep.'

They sang it together in comfort, and not long after in happiness. Golo left off playing. When the vibrations of the strings died away, Mouche went to sleep, the heads of Carrot Top and Mr Reynardo still cradled to her breasts. The cigarette glowed yet a while longer and then was extinguished. Darkness and quiet fell over the Citroën and its strangely assorted inhabitants.

Inextinguishable was the hatred that Capitaine Coq felt for the drab he had taken to his bed and soon he pushed her from the room, and lay there cursing helplessly, what or why he did not know, except it was the thought of Mouche, her simplicity, her gentleness, her inviolability and the impossibility of reducing her to the state of the woman he had just flung from his bed.

Yet the next day, life returned once more to Carrot Top and Mr Reynardo and all the others. Mouche again appeared before the booth to look after, abet and interpret them to the children, large and small, infant and adult that came to look and listen.

The tour was continued, but with a change. Thereafter, Capitaine Coq took a second room for Mouche when they stayed overnight, and avoided contact with her as much as possible.

And there was yet another difference, but this was more gradual in developing when they worked their way down through Annecy and Grenoble, heading for the south of France as the weather began to turn crisp and chill. The nature of the performance was changing.

More and more the stereotyped plot was abandoned, and the characters and the story wandered off into flights of imagination stemming from the schemes of Mr Reynardo, the streak of poetry and imagination in Carrot Top and Mouche's unique ability to enter into their make-believe instantly.

If they remained in a town for a week, a trip to the moon organised by Carrot Top with Dr Duclos as scientific director might occupy them during the entire stay, with the result that people came back again and again to see how the affair was progressing, whether Gigi and Madame Muscat had succeeded in getting themselves taken along, and how Mouche was making out with Mr Reynardo who had a dishonest scheme for merchandising pieces of the moon as souvenirs.

Again, the troupe appealed even more intimately to small communities where it played, by means of local gossip which seemed to collect astonishingly in the vicinity of the puppet booth to the end that Carrot Top might call conspiratorially:

'Psst — Mouche — Reynardo. Come here. But don't tell the girls. I know a secret . . .'

Mouche would move in closer, her plain face illuminated with excitement. 'A secret. I love secrets. Oh, Carrots, tell me at once and I won't pass it on to a soul . . .'

With his bogus smile, Reynardo would insinuate, 'Is there anything in it? Don't be a fool, Carrots. Tell me, maybe we can sell it —'

Carrots would protest, 'Oh Rey, it isn't *that* kind of a secret. It won't keep forever. In fact, it won't keep much longer. I understand that Renée Duval, the wife of Carpenter Duval back there in the audience, is expecting a little addition . . .'

Reynardo would yap, 'What? Why, they were only just married. Wait — let me count . . .' and lifting one paw he would pretend to tick off the months, 'September, October, November . . . etc.,' until Mouche would go over and stop him with, 'Reynardo – you mustn't. That's none of your business.'

Then for the next few minutes while the audience roared they would discuss the sex of the expected one; Dr Duclos learnedly and stuffily discussed biology, Madame Muscat gave advice, Ali offered himself as baby sitter. Through the magic of Mouche's personality, the villagers were swept into the middle of these odd doings and made a part of them.

Mouche was particularly adept at singling out wide-eyed children in the audience and summoning them over to meet the members of the cast, to shake hands with Ali to prove how harmless he was, stroke Mr Reynardo and converse with Carrot Top. They were unique, and the parts of France through which they made their way were not long in discovering it. The reputation of the talking and singing puppets and the live girl who stood out front and conversed with them was beginning to precede them and when they reached Nice on the Côte d'Azur it had an effect that was to be far-reaching upon all of them.

PART THREE

Moving south they remained for ten days in Lyon for the big October Fair, pressed on to Marseille and Toulon, then ventured to rim the Côte d'Azur, the strip along the Mediterranean devoted to the wealthy, and in Nice joined up with a large circus playing in a vacant lot not far from the seashore. They set up on the Midway as part of the sideshows. The rich came slumming from the big hotels, paused momentarily by the booth and were unable to tear themselves away.

The morning of the final day of the circus which was then going on to Monte Carlo, a fat, untidy looking old gentleman with a veined nose, the calculating eyes of a pig, wearing a bowler hat and carrying a gold headed cane, bustled up to Golo at the booth and demanded to see the proprietor.

The family was having its morning breakfast get-together meeting before the day's performances began and which counted as a kind of warm-up during which plans for the day were discussed.

The old gentleman was immediately greeted by

Carrot Top's shrill, 'Did you have an appointment?' and Reynardo's yapping laugh, 'First he's got to have an appointment to make an appointment. That's my department. Who did you say you thought you were?'

Gigi bobbed up and sniggered unpleasantly, 'Oh, I thought maybe it was somebody handsome.'

Madame Muscat took her turn and reprimanded her. 'Don't be a fool, Gigi. He's sure to be wealthy. Look at the fat on him. You don't get all that lard on your bones when there is a hole in your pocket.'

It was obvious that the old fellow wasn't making a very good impression on the troupe and Mouche apologised for them politely, 'They're being very naughty today. You must forgive them. Perhaps I can help you.'

It then turned out that he was an agent named Bosquet who booked acts for the Théâtre du Vaudeville in Nice, and he wished to negotiate for the troupe to appear on the stage in the show as one of the turns.

The news threw the entire collection of puppets into a kind of frenzy of excitement, joy, worry, advice and counter advice, plans and questions with Mr Reynardo yapping hysterically and thumping back and forth across the counter shouting, 'I'm going to be an actor. At last my true worth has been recognised. Ha, ha, it was me gave you the idea, wasn't it, Bosquet old boy? Mouche, did you hear? We're all going on the stage. I want to play Cyrano. I've got just the nose for it . . .'

It was a somewhat harrowing experience for Monsieur Bosquet who was made to show his credentials by Dr Duclos and submit to an interview on the state of the morals of the theatre conducted by Madame Muscat, and then deal with Monsieur Nicholas and Carrot Top so that in the end he became confused into paying more for the act than he had intended.

He never did get to see Capitaine Coq, for when the contract was completed, Carrot Top took it below and returned with the document signed. Monsieur Bosquet then tried to make up for this by inviting Mouche to dine with him, for her thin somewhat ungainly form, wide mouth and luscious eyes beneath the dark hair suddenly stirred him.

He was routed in confusion when Mr Reynardo appeared, leaning on one elbow and regarding him sardonically as he grated, 'Why you dirty, dirty old man. At your age! Aren't you ashamed of yourself going after a baby, you with all those hairs growing out of your ears? I know what YOU'RE after.'

On the other side of the stage Madame Muscat with her arms akimbo snorted, 'I suspected you from the first. I said so to Dr Duclos. What are you prepared to give her if she goes with you, diamonds, furs, a car, perhaps, hein? Not you, you old skinflint . . . Don't listen to him, my dear. I know the kind . . .'

Monsieur Bosquet fled while Reynardo roared with laughter.

The three weeks they took to prepare their act for the variety stage were not happy ones for Mouche, for while the rehearsals were as usual conducted by Carrot Top and Dr Duclos, the sudden rise in the fortunes of the troupe seemed to have made Capitaine Coq more bitter and violent than ever. Aware that their engagement was only due to the catalytic presence of Mouche, he felt compelled to resent more than ever the fact that he owed to her an affluence and position he had never known before.

For some reason he had decided to abandon their successful formula and return to the puppet play they had given in the early days, and even the puppets appeared listless and seemed to respond mechanically to something in which they had long ago lost interest.

And so he was always at Mouche when they were together afterwards, for her speech, her appearance, her country origins, endlessly reminding her, 'I picked you up out of the gutter. When will you learn something better?' He criticised her walk, her clothes, her voice. It seemed as though he was almost determined to make their debut on the stage a failure.

But if so he was doomed to disappointment and had forgotten the strange independent will of the seven dolls and the electric relationship that existed between them and the girl.

For the first performance on any stage of Capitaine Coq and his Family opened riotously on a Saturday evening to a packed house and, as with the first appearance of Mouche, the puppets individually and collectively threw away the script, so to speak, and for twenty minutes furnished the audience with entertainment that verged from the hilarious, when Mr Reynardo attempted to make himself up as Cyrano, to the touching, when Alifanfaron suffered an attack of stage fright.

They were presented against a set of a village square, with Golo strumming his guitar to attract a crowd, but with the first appearance of Carrot Top and his excitement and delight at discovering the audience and his shrill shouts for Mouche to come and see, all pretence of giving an orderly show was abandoned and everyone, including Mouche, did exactly as they pleased.

Coq had originally provided a vulgar costume for Mouche. She came on instead in a simple skirt and peasant blouse, as natural as she was, her short-cut black hair and huge eyes shining in the spotlights that picked out the booth.

The puppets illuminated the theatre with their excitement at being on a stage. They brought on embarrassed stage hands and electricians whom Mouche at once put at ease, they attempted horribly garbled snatches from French classics, they made Mouche describe the members of the orchestra whom they could not see, they demanded different coloured spotlights; they upset all tradition in a dozen different ways.

And as usual, Mouche forgot where she was and even who, and became the innocent and marvelling playmate of the seven, and so carried them all straight to the hearts of the audience.

But while laughter ruled, the highlight was touched perhaps when Alifanfaron at the first sight of so large an audience froze into such a ludicrous and stammering attack of stage fright that not even Mouche could coax him out of it!

Golo strolled on out of the wings, plucking at his guitar. He chuckled and said in his soft, rich, African French, 'Some time when you scared, it helps if you sing your scare away.'

His fingers created the notes he had once played for Mouche on a certain night long ago in far off Besançon. The girl picked up the thread at once. She went to the big, stupid giant, trembling and cowering in the booth, and put her arm about him, and rocking him gently sang with Golo:

'My young one, my sweeting,
      Rock in you cradle —
   The sea rocks your father . . .'

Carrot Top came up and joined in the chorus, and at the end the giant lifted his shaggy head, gazed out to all quarters of the audience and announced ineffably, 'I'm not scared any more.' Carrot Top bounced over and patted Golo's cheek and kissed Mouche. The house was as hushed as though it had been a church. Many in the audience were crying.

The next moment, Mouche and Reynardo were romping through their own version of '*Va t'en*,' with Gigi the eternal soubrette and later Madame Muscat and Dr Duclos.

In the wings, during the performance, there stood a young man in blue tights with gold spangles and an overcoat thrown over his shoulders. Never once did he take his large, moist, handsome brown eyes from the face and figure of the girl by the puppet booth.

His name was Balotte, and he was an acrobat, a member of a troupe waiting to go onto the high trapeze in the turn that followed the puppet number. Other artists were likewise gathered there to watch the new act and find themselves as captivated as the audience.

But Balotte, who was a good, simple boy of somewhat limited intelligence and overweening vanity, was for the first time in his life falling in love with someone other than himself.

Looking out onto the stage at this gentle, gay, sincere and motherly girl, he felt his heart touched as it had never been before. Yet at the same time he was filled with a professional's excitement at the show she was giving, for he appreciated what a girl who could make an audience sit up and take notice like that could do for him. He had long had it in his mind to go as a single and had been looking for a girl partner to throw him the handkerchief and stand about while he performed his feats.

The act came to a close to ear-shattering applause. Wave after wave of it poured over Mouche. She brought on each of the puppets for a bow. When the curtain closed upon her for the last time, she was standing with her back to the booth. Carrot Top had his cheek pressed against one of hers, an arm about her neck, Mr Reynardo the other. Her eyes were shining. She had never been so happy.

When she came off, Balotte went to her and said, '*Hola*, little one. that was not bad, and I have seen many acts. Now stay here and watch me too. Afterwards I will have something to say to you.'

And so, out of politeness, Mouche remained in the wings and looked upwards at the handsome boy as he swung, leaped, whirled and somersaulted with his partners and occasionally threw her a look as he sat resting on the trapeze high up in the flies or brushed his moustache self-consciously.

Capitaine Coq came by, clad in black corduroy trousers and black high-necked sweater emphasising his pallor, his fox-coloured hair and the cold glitter of his eyes. It was a commentary on his art that outside of the stage manager, hardly anyone knew who he was. He paused for a moment and followed Mouche's glance upwards. 'Kinkers,' he sneered, using the showman's derogatory term for acrobats, and spat. Then without another glance at Mouche he went on. He had made a date with a girl in the orchestra who played the flute. Now that he was becoming a success, it was time, he thought, to try it on with someone with a little class.

But Balotte, when he came sliding down the rope, was pleased, though not surprised, that Mouche had remained there watching him and said, 'Well? All right, little one?'

Mouche replied sincerely, 'Oh yes, indeed. I thought you were wonderful.'

'Oh, that wasn't anything. Wait until you see the new routine I am working up. Something really sensational.'

'But isn't it fearfully dangerous?' Mouche asked. 'Without a net or anything?'

Balotte preened himself. 'But of course. That is what the public likes. See here, what about coming out with me for something to eat and a glass of beer?'

He was amazed at the expression of panic that crossed Mouche's face. 'I . . . I don't know whether I can. I've never been before . . .'

Balotte came quickly to the point. 'Is he your husband, that one? The fellow who calls himself Capitaine Coq?' he asked.

Mouche shook her head quickly. 'Oh no. He is not.'

Balotte was intelligent enough not to inquire any further. 'Well then, put on your street clothes and I'll meet you inside the stage door as soon as I have changed.'

It was several minutes before Mouche could bring herself to believe that she was free to accept such an invitation. The bondage in which Capitaine Coq held her had become almost a habit, but even more, she belonged to the seven dolls and felt as though she ought to have asked Carrot Top for permission.

She hurried then to keep the rendezvous but found herself wishing she might have discussed with Madame Muscat the propriety of going out with a young man who had just introduced himself to her.

Balotte arrived shortly, hair sleeked down, the inevitable acrobat's white silk scarf around his neck inside his jacket, and smelling faintly of perspiration mingled with liniment.

He was delighted by his success and flashed magnificent white teeth at her. Also he took her most solicitously by the arm to guide her as though she were fragile. It had been so long since a man had been gentle with her that it quite warmed Mouche's heart. All of a sudden she remembered that she was a young girl and laughed happily and leaning on the sturdy arm of the young man asked, 'Where shall we go?'

They went to a water-front café at the far end of the Quai du Midi.

There, sitting out under the stars they supped on highly seasoned bouillabaisse which called for quantities of beer which in turn made them light-headed and merry.

They danced together and contact with this strange girl made Balotte quite ardent and he held her close, but yet tenderly. The tenderness found an answering response in Mouche. Youth was wooing youth. For the first time in longer than she could remember, Mouche was enjoying herself in a normal manner. She felt as though she could never have enough of this magic night.

Everything was heightened, the sparkle of her eyes, the glitter of the stars, the swing of the music, the movement of her limbs, and of course the good looks of Balotte and the impression he was making.

Indeed, she was almost insatiable for innocent pleasure and did not wish to go home. Balotte, certain that it was his person and enthralling tales about his triumphs in the circus and variety world and his plans for future successes that made her so happy and gay, humoured her, for he was enjoying himself too. When at four in the morning the café finally closed, they were the last to leave.

Balotte, for all his vanity, came of a good circus family, and therefore, in love as he felt himself to be with Mouche, was respectful of her and honourable in his attentions towards another in his own profession. He took her home on a tram and left her at the door of her hotel with no more than a warm pressure of the hand and a loving look from his dark liquid eyes.

When Mouche went inside she found Capitaine Coq in the lobby waiting for her. He was slumped in a chair in the dingy, ill-smelling lobby, a cigarette hanging from his lip, but he was sober. The flute-player had proved flabby, damp, self-accusing and had drenched him with tears. His temper was even more vile than usual and he took it out on Mouche.

He said, 'Come over here. Where the devil have you been? You'll be getting a regular salary now. You don't have to go out whoring in the streets.'

Mouche felt hatred of this man so intensely that she thought she would become ill or faint. Yet the small taste of freedom she had enjoyed, the echoes of the innocent evening enabled her to face him. She replied, 'I was out with Balotte. He asked me to have supper with him.'

Coq laughed harshly. 'Until four in the morning? That kind of dining we know . . .'

'It is not true. We were dancing. Why shouldn't I dance with him? He is kind to me.'

Capitaine Coq got up out of his chair, his hands and face working with rage. He ground his teeth and took her by the wrist so that she cried out with pain.

'That, and more of it,' he shouted at her, applying more pressure. 'If ever I catch you with that walking sweat gland again, I'll smash every bone in your body and in his too. Remember. Now get up to your room.'

At the performance the next day Dr Duclos of all people came up with a present for Mouche. It appeared he had been shopping and, passing a perfume counter, had so far abandoned caution as to invest in a small flacon. Oddly, it was the first perfume Mouche had ever had. They made her open it and try it on; Gigi jealously sampled some, Madame Muscat sniffed disdainfully, Ali tried to drink it because if it smelled so good it must taste better. For twenty minutes they elaborated this slender theme to the enchantment of the audience and ended with Mr Reynardo in Mouche's arms quite overcome and swooning.

As Mouche came offstage, Balotte, waiting to go on, whispered, 'Tonight again?'

Mouche looked about her in alarm. 'I don't dare. He has threatened to do you an injury.'

Balotte snorted, 'Ho! I can take care of myself. I know of a place where the music is even better. Be at the stage door again the same time, little one, eh . . .?'

Mouche replied, 'I don't know.'

But she was there, hoping that Coq would not be about. She longed so for the gaiety and the sweet ease of being with someone who was kind. She did not have to wait. Balotte was there. And Capitaine Coq stepped out of a shadowed corner.

Capitaine Coq said, 'Well, I can see that you both are asking for it. Have it then!' He whipped the backs of five bony fingers across Mouche's face, knocking her up against the wall. 'Gutter slut!' he bawled at her.

Balotte made a menacing movement. Coq turned on him, 'As for you, you muscle-bound idiot, you can hang by your tail like a monkey, but you wouldn't lift a finger for her or anybody else. I'm going to teach you to keep away from her.'

But Capitaine Coq was wrong. Balotte was no coward and furthermore he had a body like iron, wrists of steel and more than a little knowledge of the science of attack and defence.

The fight was short and savage, both men moiling, writhing and striking in silence with no sound but the whistling of their breathing, the thud of blows and the grunts of pain. Then it was over with Capitaine Coq lying in a battered, bloodied heap upon the floor, stunned, whipped and unable to rise. He was bleeding from the nose and mouth and a gash in his cheek, and one eye was closing.

With his red hair, crinkled pale face and black suit, he was the personification of the devil dethroned, evil conquered by good, as the young acrobat stood over him panting, but unmarked. He was the villain foiled, the wicked bully who at last receives his just deserts. He lay in an untidy heap like a horrid insect that has been squashed.

Mouche stood by the wall, her hand to her own bruised lips, staring down at him. So had she prayed to see him, beaten, cowed, mastered. Yet she was conscious only of being filled with sadness and of an ache in her throat comparable to those experienced sometimes before the puppet booth when one or the other of its inhabitants was particularly moving. She had not known that a wish fulfilled could be so empty and that the physical destruction of the object of her hatred would yield no more than the desire to weep for the downfall of evil.

Balotte moved over to him, prepared to kick him unconscious if need be, and asked, 'Want any more?'

The glassy eyes of Capitaine Coq filled with venom, but he shook his head, mumbling something unintelligible and did not attempt to get up.

Balotte said, 'Come along then, Mouche. This fellow won't give you any more trouble.'

They went out then arm in arm and Mouche did not look back at the heap on the floor, for had she done so, she could not have gone. This time they did not dance – as if by mutual understanding they recognised it was not the time – but instead sat in a corner booth, eating and getting acquainted. And under the stimulus of the youth and wooing of Balotte, Mouche's mood of sorrow evaporated. They walked home and stood for a while by the promenade looking out over the harbour with Nice's necklace of lights curving away from them and the stars cascading over the black, frowning wall of the mountains behind the city. Balotte kissed her and, gratefully, Mouche returned his kisses.

At the next performance of Capitaine Coq and his Family, Carrot Top appeared with a black eye and was raucously greeted by Mr Reynardo and the rest of the cast demanding to know how it had happened, with Carrot Top insisting that he had walked into a door in the dark. They devoted the act to discussing the truth of this plus the best remedies, Madame Muscat finally arriving with a small piece of filet which Mouche solicitously bound to the optic. All through the show she felt herself unaccountably close to tears. Yet she was glad for the pressure of Balotte's hand as she passed him and he whispered, 'Petite Mouche, tonight we dance.'

This was the night too that the manager of the theatre stood at the door and counted more than two hundred patrons who had been there the week before and who had returned to see what mischief the family of Capitaine Coq were up to.

As the second month of the engagement drew to a close and it was obvious that the puppet show was as popular as ever and a decided drawing card, the management decided to retain them, but change the rest of the bill. This meant that amongst others, the company of aerialists of which Balotte was a member, would be moving on.

One night, therefore, a little more than a week before this was to take place, as they sat on their favourite bench on the sea promenade and watched the moon set, Balotte asked Mouche to marry him and was accepted.

'You will see,' he had said, 'as my assistant in my new act, you will make me famous, and yourself too. We will tour the world together.'

But also he had told her that he loved her.

Mouche responded to his sincerity and his gentleness. She had been happy during those weeks that Balotte had been courting her. Against the normality of their relationship and his simplicity, the walks they took together, the picnic lunches in the hills, the nightmare of her relationship to Capitaine Coq could be recognised and Mouche knew that an end must be made to it. She was sure that she loved Balotte, for he was handsome, kind and sympathetic to her and there was no reason why she should not.

It had been a particularly trying week for Mouche for although, since the beating, while Coq had offered her no further violence, or tried to interfere with her dates with Balotte, he was bitter and sneering and his tongue had never been nastier as he took her to task before stage hands and performers. His movements became more and more mysterious. Sometimes she would not see him for a whole day. Then the next he seemed always at her elbow, biting, mocking, sardonic or abusive.

It was said that he would spend long hours sitting in the puppet booth in silence, and once the night-watchman making his rounds in the theatre between the hours of midnight and eight when the charwoman came, swore that he heard the voices of the puppets coming from the booth in some kind of argument, but by the time he made his way from the balcony to the stage there seemed to be no one there, and only the empty gloves of the Reynardo and Gigi puppets were found lying on the counter of the booth.

Capitaine Coq received the news of Mouche's forthcoming marriage and departure from the show with surprising calmness. Perhaps he had been expecting it. They went to him together, for Mouche had not the courage to face him alone. She declared her intention of remaining with the show until the end of the month when the contract expired. Then she and Balotte would be married and she would leave.

He had listened to her with a curious expression on his cynical countenance and then had simply shrugged and turned away, vanishing in the direction of his dressing-room which was on the other side of the stage from that occupied by Mouche. And thereafter for the remainder of the engagement she never saw him again.

But if Coq appeared to accept Mouche's decision to marry Balotte and leave the act with a certain amount of resignation, the seven little creatures whom Mouche met twice daily in the pool of spotlights focused on the shabby little puppet booth onstage, took the event over, discussed it and harped on it endlessly.

Each reacted according to his or her nature to Mouche's romance and engagement, and Madame Muscat's attempts to ascertain whether Mouche knew the facts of life and her advice to her for her wedding night was one of the most hilarious evenings the old theatre had ever known.

Day after day Mouche went through some kind of catechism, with regard to her plans and her future. Where would she go, where would she live, where was she going to be married? Gigi wanted to know about her trousseau, and Dr Duclos gave a pompous pseudo-scientific lecture on genetics and just why her children were likely to be acrobats. Mr Reynardo tried to get the catering job for the wedding and Alifanfaron applied for the job of nurse.

Yet, to anyone witnessing one or more of these performances, it became evident that for all of the childish interest and seeming light-hearted banter, the fact of Mouche's approaching marriage and departure hung over them filled with the tragic implications of children about to lose the security of the presence of one who was both loved and loving.

Through every show, there ran a vein of dread of the day, a forlornness, a helplessness and a dumb pleading that wrung Mouche's heart, for with her departure becoming imminent, she herself did not know how she would be able to leave these little people who in the past year had become such a part of her and the only real friends, companions and playmates she had ever known.

Often, while Mouche would be in conversation with one character, another would appear from below, retire to the end of the booth, stare, silently and longingly at her, then heave a large sigh and vanish again. The pressure upon Mouche was becoming intolerable and she did not know how she would be able to reach the final night without breaking, for Balotte could not help her. He was pleased with the publicity that had come his way and the applause that greeted his appearances now that he was the bridegroom-to-be in a romantic story that had been written up in the newspapers. He had no idea of what was happening to Mouche.

The final performance of Capitaine Coq and his Family which took place in the Théâtre du Vaudeville on the Saturday night of December 15th, was one that Mouche would not forget as long as she lived.

The old theatre with its red velvet drapes, gold-encrusted boxes and shimmering candelabra had been sold out for more than a week. Word had spread along the Côte d'Azur, and there were visitors from Cannes, St Tropez, Antibes and Monaco. Half of the audience present were regulars who had fallen in love over the weeks with Mouche, or the seven dolls, and who had paid premiums to be there. The front rows sparkled with jewels and décolletage and white shirt fronts. The playboys and playgirls of the gold coast had a wonderful nose for the unusual, the slightly *amer*, the bitter-sweet in entertainment, the story behind the story, the broken heart palpitating onstage for all to see. The gossip had gone around the cocktail circuit, 'My dear, it's frightfully amusing. She talks with all these little dolls, but there's supposed to be the most fantastic man behind them. No

one has ever seen him. He's supposed to be madly in love
with her. Philippe has four tickets. We're all driving
over and dining at the Casino first.'

It began as usual with the strains of 'Va t'en, va t'en'
dying away in the orchestra pit, followed by curtain rise
showing a corner of the village square with the puppet
booth set up, and Golo, the white patch gleaming over
his vacant eye socket, strumming his guitar in front of it
in a little song dedicated to calling the village folk
together to see their show.

The spotlight on Golo would dim; the light pools by
the booth would narrow. One of the puppets would
appear with startling suddenness in the limelight and
claim the attention of all. Mouche was never onstage as
the curtain went up.

This night it began with Mr Reynardo making a
furtive appearance on the counter of the booth, looking
carefully to the right and left and behind him as well.
Then he called: 'Pssssst! Golo!' And when Golo appeared
from behind the booth, 'Where's Mouche?'

'I don't know, Mr Reynardo. You want me to call
her?'

'In a minute. I've got something for her.' He ducked
down and appeared with a handsome red fox fur scarf,
tipped with a bushy tail at one end and a small fox mask
at the other. He stretched it along the counter and for a
moment snuffled up and down its length. 'It's for her,'
he told Golo.

'Dieu!' remarked Golo, 'but that's rich. I'll go fetch Mouche, Mr Reynardo.'

While Golo went off into the wings, Mr Reynardo scrutinised the scarf closely. 'Eeeeeh!' he said with some slight distaste. 'Awfully familiar. Say, she was a nice-looking babe . . . I seem to remember her from somewhere.' He moved up to the head of the scarf and bestowed a surprisingly gentle kiss onto the muzzle of the fox mask. 'Requiescat in pace, kid,' he said. 'And keep Mouche warm.'

Mouche walked onstage into a storm of applause that lasted for several minutes and brought the ache back to her throat. Whenever she was shown kindness or approval it brought her close to tears.

At last she was able to proceed. She began, 'Golo said you were looking for me, Rey . . .'

'Uhuh. Glad you got here before the others. Er . . . ah . . .' The fox was looking not entirely comfortable. He reached and taking the scarf in his jaws he held it out to the girl. 'This is for you. It's a wed – ' he seemed to gag over the word and switched, '. . . a going-away present for you.'

Mouche's hand flew to her heart. 'Oh Rey! How beautiful. Oh, you shouldn't have . . . You know you shouldn't have spent so much . . .'

Her expression altered suddenly to the wise, tender and slightly admonishing, 'Mother-knows-all-what-have-you-done-now' look that her audiences knew so well. 'Rey! Come over here to me at once and tell me where you got that beautiful and expensive scarf . . .'

The fox squirmed slightly. 'Must I, Mouche?'

'Reynardo! You know what I have always told you about being honest . . .'

By a twist of his neck Mr Reynardo managed to achieve a look of injured innocence. 'Well, if you must know, I bought it on the hire purchase instalment plan.'

'Indeed. And what happens if you fail to keep up the payments? Oh Rey! I suppose they'll come to my home and take it away from me . . .'

The fox slowly shook his head. 'Oh no . . . You see, I made a kind of deal.'

Mouche was mock serious now and once more lost in their make-believe. She knew the kind of sharp practice to which he was prone. She asked, 'And pray what kind of a deal, Mr Reynardo?'

'We-e-ell . . . If I fail to keep up the instalments the man gets something else in exchange. I signed a paper. It's all settled.'

Mouche walked right into the trap. 'Did you? And just what is he to have in exchange for this exquisite fur piece?'

The fox appeared to swallow once, then modestly turned his head aside before he replied meekly, 'Me.'

Struck to the heart, Mouche cried, 'Oh my dear! You mean you're pawned yourself . . . Oh Rey . . . I don't know what to say . . .'

For a moment Mouche glanced out across the footlights and the balcony spot picked up two drops of light traversing her cheeks and splintered them so that they glowed like diamonds.

Like a flash the fox was across the stage of the booth and whipped his red, furry head with the black mask and long nose into the hollow of Mouche's shoulder and snuggled there with a contented sigh in the manner of a naughty child that takes immediate advantage of any tenderness.

The contact came close to breaking Mouche's heart, for love of this sly, wicked little creature whose mischief and amorality stemmed from the fact that it was his nature and he did not know any better. Yet he tried hard to please her and be honest for her sake.

Thereafter, the other puppets appeared to delight and torture Mouche still further with their parting gifts and little made-up awkwardly sincere speeches.

Dr Duclos presented her with an encyclopaedia. 'Everything I know is inside this book,' the formally dressed penguin pontificated. 'Thought you might like to have it handy for information on all subjects when I am not around any longer.'

Gigi gave her a trousseau negligée and nightgown set and a grudging kiss, while Madame Muscat handed her a rolling-pin and an egg beater, remarking significantly, 'A marriage can be kept in order with these, my dear. And remember, all men are beasts, but neces-

sary ones.' From Alifanfaron she received a photograph
of himself, and Monsieur Nicholas gave her an oddly
turned piece of wood that was not one but many
shapes.

'For your first-born,' he said. 'It is a toy I have made
for him that is not any, yet is still all toys, for in his
imagination, when he plays with it, it will be whatever
he sees in it, or wishes it to be.'

Golo came forward. He had a little African good-luck
God he had carved for her out of a piece of ebon wood.
Like the white-shafted spotlights beamed down from
above, the emotions and tensions of everyone in the
theatre seemed concentrated on this one spot, the
shabby little booth, the negro with the gleaming
patch over one eye who was crying unashamedly, and
the girl who was trying desperately to hold herself
together.

From where she was standing, Mouche could look
into the wings and see the showgirls, singers, dancers,
acrobats and stage hands gathered there, watching and
listening, as spellbound as the audience. She saw Balotte
in his blue spangled tights, his beautiful body proud and
erect, and he looked like a stranger to her.

Carrot Top appeared alone contriving to look more
worried and forlorn than usual. He was empty-handed.
He tried to appear nonchalant by whistling, but it soon
petered out when his lips seemed to have trouble
pursing themselves for the whistle. Finally, he gave it up,

saying, 'Oh, what's the use. I'm not fooling anybody. I came to say goodbye, Mouche.'

Mouche said, 'Goodbye, dear Carrot Top.'

'Will you miss me?'

'Oh yes, Carrot Top. I shall miss you terribly.'

'Shall you be having children of your own, Mouche?'

'Yes . . .'

'Will they be like us?'

'Oh I hope so . . . I do hope so . . .'

Carrot Top was silent a moment and then said, 'I didn't get you anything. I couldn't. I'll give you my love to take with you, Mouche . . .'

Now the ache was closing her throat again. 'Carrot Top! Do you really love me?' In all the time they had been together, he had never once said it.

The puppet nodded. 'Oh yes. I always have. Only you never noticed. Never mind. It's too late now. Mouche, will you give *me* a going-away present?'

'Oh yes, Carrots. Anything I have . . .'

'Will you sing a song with me?'

'Of course, Carrots. What shall it be?'

The little doll said, 'Golo knows.'

The Senegalese appeared and picked out an introduction on his guitar. It was the Breton lullaby. Mouche had not expected this. She did not know whether she could get through it.

Carrot Top held out his hand to her and she took it in both hers. They sang:

[147]

> 'My young one, my sweeting,
>   Rock in your cradle,
> The storm winds are blowing,
>   God rules the storm winds . . .'

When they had finished, Golo wandered away quietly into the wings and Carrot Top reached up and kissed Mouche's cheek.

'Don't forget us when you have children of your own, Mouche.' He vanished beneath the counter.

The others came whipping up by twos, to cry, 'Don't forget us, Mouche,' and overwhelm her with pecks and kisses.

Mouche, her eyes now blinded by tears, opened her arms and cried to them as though there was no one else there but they and she, 'Oh no, no! I can never forget you. My darlings, I will never forget you. You will always be like my own children and as dear to me . . .'

She hardly heard the band swing into their closing theme, or the heavy swish of the descending curtains, closing them out from the tempest of applause and cheers from the audience out front. The last thing that Mouche saw and heard was Mr Reynardo, his muzzle turned skyward, howling like a coyote and Alifanfaron with his head buried in the folds of the side curtains of the puppet booth.

Then she fled to her dressing-room, locked the door and putting her head down on her arms, wept. Nor could she be persuaded by knocks or shouts from without to open the door and emerge to take her bows. She felt as though she would cry endlessly for the rest of her life.

She would not open even when Balotte came to fetch her and begged him to go, promising to meet him at his hotel in the morning and, finally, he too departed.

She remained sitting in the dark of her dressing-room for a long while.

On every stage in the world at night after the performance is over, there stands a single, naked electric light bulb. No spot seems as glaring as where the incandescence sheds its halo, no shadows as long and deep and grotesque as those lurking at the bulb's extreme range, spilling over flats and props, pieces of sets and furniture.

Against the brick rear wall of the theatre, almost at the farthest edge of the illumination, yet visible, stood the deserted puppet booth, its white oil-cloth sign 'Capitaine Coq et sa Famille' barely legible.

Unseen in the shadows, squatting on his haunches, Golo sorrowed alone in the dark in the manner of his people. It was nearly four o'clock in the morning, and the theatre was empty.

Mouche slipped from her dressing-room for the last time. She carried a small dressing-case in which she had packed her few personal belongings. Her wardrobe she was leaving behind her just as she was leaving a part of herself behind, the Mouche that had been and would never be again.

To reach the stage door it was necessary for her to cross the dark, cavernous stage. From the passageway she stepped into the wings beyond the range of the single light that would have guided her across. And out of this darkness a hand reached and grasped her by the wrist and another was placed across her mouth before she could cry out with the fright that momentarily stopped her heart.

Had the distant light reflected upon the pale, hate-ravaged features and red hair of Capitaine Coq, Mouche's heart might never have started beating again.

But the hard calluses on the fingers covering her lips told their story and a gleam of white eyeballs completed the identification.

Golo whispered into her ear, 'For the love of the dear God, do not make a sound.'

As quietly, Mouche asked against the pounding of her heart, 'What is it, Golo?'

'I don't know. Something is happening. Stay here with me, Miss Mouche, but make no noise. Golo very much afraid.'

He pulled her gently down to her knees beside him and she could feel that he was trembling.

'But, Golo . . .'

'Shhhhh, Miss Mouche. Don't speak. Listen . . .'

At first there was no sound but their own soft

breathing. Then there came a faint rustling and scratching. It appeared to come from somewhere near the centre of the stage. Sight came to the aid of straining ears and Golo pressed Mouche's hand hard with his as the head of Carrot Top rose slowly above the counter of the puppet booth and reconnoitred carefully.

There was something horrible in the caution with which he looked to the right and to the left, and then with that extraordinarily life-like movement with which he was endowed, leaned out from the ends of the booth and gazed behind as well; horrible too was the fact no one was supposed to be there, that the performance was to an empty theatre, or perhaps even more horrible still that it was no performance at all . . .

Golo whispered, 'He gone away early, but *they* came back. I knew they were here. I felt it.'

It was Mouche's turn to quiet him and she pressed his arm gently and said, 'Shhhhhhhh.'

Having made certain there was no one about, Carrot Top retired to the far end of the counter and let his face sink into his hands and remained thus for a minute or two.

Then the quiet was disturbed by a rasping, gravelly whisper: 'That you up there, Carrots?'

The red-headed puppet slowly lifted his head from his hands, looked down deliberately and replied, 'Yes.'

'Is the coast clear?'

'Yes. There's nobody here.'

'Where's the watchman?'

'Asleep in the boiler-room.'

The head of the sharp-faced fox arose from below. He too reconnoitred for a moment, then, satisfied, leaned on the counter at the opposite end from Carrot Top. Finally, the leprechaun said in a listless and woebegone voice, 'Well, what do we do now?'

Reynardo sighed, then replied, 'I don't know if you don't. You've been running the show, Carrot Top. Kind of messed it up, didn't you, old fellow?'

Carrot Top reflected. 'Did I? I suppose I did. I never thought she'd leave us for that knuckle-head. She'll never be happy with him.'

'Why didn't you tip her off?'

'Madame Muscat tried, but it was no use. She's too young to see that monkey will never think of anyone but himself.'

'Is she really going to marry him, Carrot Top?'

'Oh yes. It's all over.'

The fox said, '*Merde!*'

Carrot Top reproved him. 'Oh, cut it out, Rey. It won't help to use bad language. You know how *she* hated it. The thing is we've got to decide what to do. Is there any use in going on?'

Mr Reynardo replied quickly, 'Not as far as I'm concerned. She was the only thing I ever cared about. I'm ready to call it a day.'

'Me too. I suppose we ought to put it to a vote.'

'Uhuh. Take the chair, Carrots. I'll call the roll. Ali . . .?'

The voice of the giant came from below the counter. 'I'm here, I think.'

'Dr Duclos?'

'Present.'

'Gigi?'

'Yes.'

'Madame Muscat?'

'Of course.'

'Monsieur Nicholas?'

'Yes, yes.'

Mr Reynardo said, 'All present and accounted for.' And folded his arms.

Carrot Top then made a little speech in a not too firm voice. 'Ladies and gentlemen of our company. Inasmuch as our well loved sister Mouche has left us to be married and will never return, I have called this meeting to decide what is to be done. The question before the committee of the whole is: Shall we try to continue without her?'

Dr Duclos commented, 'What's the use if nobody comes to see us, Mr Chairman?'

Reynardo turned it around, 'What's the use if we can't see her?'

Gigi's voice remarked, 'We could get someone like her to take her place.'

Alifanfaron was heard to rumble: 'Gee, I'm stupid,

but even I know there's no one like her. Nobody could take her place.'

Madame Muscat contributed, 'Well, we had a show we used to do before she came to us.'

The deep voice of Monsieur Nicholas sounded from below. 'Do you wish to return to that? And sleeping in haystacks again? One can never go back . . .'

Gigi's girlish treble inquired anxiously, 'But if there isn't anything forward?'

'Then,' replied Monsieur Nicholas, 'perhaps the best idea is to go nowhere.'

'Oh,' exclaimed Carrot Top. 'How?'

'Simply by ceasing to exist.'

Carrot Top said 'Oh' again, and Reynardo rasped, 'Ha ha, suits me.' While Dr Duclos said pompously, 'Logically sound, I must admit, however unpleasant the prospect.' Ali complained, 'I don't know what you're talking about. All I know is if I can't be with Mouche I want to die.'

Mr Reynardo sniggered, 'That's the general idea, Ali, old boy. You've hit it for once. Put it to a vote, Mr Chairman.'

There was a moment of silence. Then Carrot Top said firmly, 'All in favour of ceasing to exist say "Aye".'

There was a scattered chorus of Ayes, and one squeaky 'No' from Gigi.

Reynardo growled: 'Motion carried. Proceed, Mr Chairman.'

'Now?' Carrot Top asked. There were no dissents. He continued: 'Next question – how?'

Dr Duclos said: 'I have always been fascinated by self-immolation; the Indian custom of Suttee where the widow casts herself upon the funeral pyre of her deceased spouse . . .'

Reynardo said, 'I don't see the connection, but the idea isn't bad. Fire is clean.'

Carrot Top said: 'There's a vacant lot back of the theatre.'

Gigi suddenly wailed: 'But I don't want to die.'

Reynardo ducked down beneath the counter swiftly and came up with the half doll that was Gigi, empty, her eyes staring vacuously, clamped in his jaws. Then he carefully dropped her over the side of the booth onto the stage where she fell with a small crash that echoed shockingly through the empty theatre. 'Then live, little golden-haired pig,' he said.

Mouche drew in her breath and whispered, 'Poor, poor little Gigi . . .'

Mr Reynardo looked over the side of the booth at the little heap lying on the stage and then asked, 'Anybody else want to back out?'

Madame Muscat pronounced Gigi's epitaph: 'She was never much good anyway.'

Alifanfaron said: 'But she was so pretty.'

Carrot Top sighed briefly: 'One of the world's great illusions, the golden-haired fairy princess . . .'

[155]

'Who in the end turns out to be nothing more than a walking appetite,' Reynardo concluded, for he had never much liked Gigi.

Monsieur Nicholas said from below: 'It is not necessary to be unkind. God made her as she was, as He made us all.'

Alifanfaron asked: 'Gee, what will become of God when we are gone?'

The voice of Monsieur Nicholas replied after a moment of reflection: 'I think perhaps God will destroy Himself too if it is indeed true that He has created us all in His own image . . .'

Carrot Top asked: 'Why?'

'Because if He is God He could not bear to contemplate such a miserable failure of his designs.'

Mr Reynardo stretched his neck and looked down below the counter. 'Oh,' he said. 'That's clever of you. I hadn't thought about it in that way.'

'Most profound,' continued Dr Duclos, 'not to mention praglatic . . .'

Carrot Top corrected him almost absent-mindedly, 'Pragmatic.' He sighed then and added, 'Well, then, it's goodbye to Capitaine Coq and his Family.'

Golo turned a stricken face towards Mouche. 'They going to die. Don't let them, Miss Mouche . . .'

Mr Reynardo went over to Carrot Top and stuck out his paw. 'So long, kid. It wasn't a bad ride while it lasted.'

Carrot Top took it and shook it solemnly. 'Good-bye,

Rey. You've always been a friend. I'll go down and get things ready . . .'

Mouche arose. Her knees were stiff from kneeling, her heart was pounding with excitement and her throat was dry. She picked up her small valise and marched across the stage, her heels clicking on the boards and the single standing light picking up her slender shadow, speeding it ahead of her and throwing it as a kind of prophecy of her coming athwart the puppet booth and its single inhabitant.

It was astonishing, this repetition of the first time that Mouche had encountered the puppets of Capitaine Coq.

There was the same darkness with the single light to probe the shadows, there was the mysterious booth looming out of the shadow, the lone puppet perched on the counter, and the slender figure of a girl marching by carrying a valise.

Except, now, the shoe was on the other foot and it was Mouche who paused in the spill of yellow light before the puppet booth and called to the small figure flattened on the counter there, 'Hello, Baby . . .'

Mr Reynardo, the composed, the cynical, and the self-assured, was taken aback. His whole frame shuddered as he reared up and peered through the gloom, for he was handicapped by having to look directly into the light. His jaws moved silently several times and finally he managed to produce a croak.

'Mouche! Where have you been? Have you been around here long?'

Mouche paused before the booth and set her valise down. She contemplated the agitated and nonplussed fox jittering back and forth. Finally she said, 'Never mind where I have been. I know where you are going. There is nothing to be found in the heart of flames but the ashes of regret. I'm ashamed of you all.'

The fox stopped flapping and contemplated her long and hard. 'We didn't know you were here.' Then he added, 'We voted . . .'

'Was it a fair vote?' Mouche asked.

The fox swallowed. 'Well, maybe Monsieur Nicholas, Carrot Top and I rigged it a little. But it was only because of you – going away and leaving us, I mean.'

'And Gigi here?' Mouche bent over and picked up the empty doll.

The fox looked uneasy. He flattened his head to the counter and thereby seemed to have moved his eyes guiltily. He said, 'We pushed her out of the nest. We excommunicated her.'

'We?'

'I did. She didn't love you . . .'

'It was wrong, Rey.'

He hung his head. 'I know it. Don't leave us, Mouche.'

'Rey – you're blackmailing me again like you always have – with love . . .'

[158]

There might have been the well-dressed, attentive, cultured audience of the night before out front instead of the blank, staring empty seats; there might have been the rabble from the slums washed up from the edge of the street fair, gathered about the booth; there might have been the peasant children and the village people gathered about them on the village square — it made no difference. When the puppets were there and she talking with them, she lost herself, she lost reality, she lost the world — there remained only these, her friends and companions and their need.

The hoarse voice of the fox dropped to a rattling whisper again. 'This time it isn't blackmail, Mouche. If you must go, take me with you.'

'And leave the others? Rey, you can't desert them now.'

The wary figure of the fox stirred. He moved imperceptibly closer to where Mouche was standing. 'Oh yes, I can. I don't care about anything or anybody. Let me come, Mouche. I'm housebroken. And you know me — gentle with children.'

The old habits were so hard to break. Momentarily Mouche forgot about herself and that she had parted with all this, that this was the beginning of the morning that was to see her wedded to Balotte and a new and normal life. She went over to the booth, and bending over in her sweetly tender and concerned manner admonished, 'But don't you see, Rey, that's being disloyal.'

Mr Reynardo appeared to ponder this for a moment. Then he moved closer and barely nuzzled the tip of his snout onto the back of Mouche's hand. He sighed deeply and said: 'I know. But what's the diff? Everybody knows I'm a heel. They expect it of me. And to tell you the truth, it's a relief to be one again. I've tried to be a good fellow but it doesn't work – not unless you're around to keep me from backsliding . . .'

She could not help herself. She placed a caressing hand upon the bristly red head: 'My poor Rey . . .'

Instantly the fox whipped his head into the hollow between neck and shoulder and was whispering, 'Mouche – take care of me . . .'

The touch of him was as always an exquisitely tender agony. Her heart swelled with love for this unhappy creature. With startling suddenness Alifanfaron bobbed up.

'Oh gee, excuse me. Am I interrupting something? Goodness, it's Mouche. Are you back again, Mouche? If you're back again I don't want to die any more . . .'

The fox grated: 'Damn. Why did you have to come up just then? I nearly had her.' He vanished.

Mouche said: 'But, Ali dear, I cannot stay, I'm going to be married, and I don't want you to die . . . What shall I do?' They had all the deadly logical illogicality of children.

'Take me along, Mouche. You don't know what it is to be a giant and stupid and lose a friend . . .'

Mouche had heard herself say, 'I'm going to be married . . .' but it was like something someone else said about another person. Where was that real world now, the world of sanity and things as they ought to be to which she had been fleeing to save herself from complete destruction? Now she could remember only how she had always felt about Alifanfaron's troubles.

'Oh, Ali,' she cried, 'you're not really stupid. It's just that you were born too big in a world filled with people who are too small.'

'Ah hooom! Harrrumph! Exactly, my dear. A very trenchant remark. Most sage indeed.' It was Dr Duclos the penguin in formal attire as usual, his pince-nez attached to a black ribbon perched on the end of his beak. He peered at her for a moment and then said: 'So glad to see you're back. We've all missed you frightfully.' He went away.

Carrot Top appeared whistling a snatch of '*Va t'en, va t'en,*' and then with a simulated surprise, discovered the girl standing at her accustomed place slightly to the right of the centre of the booth. He said: 'Oh hello, Mouche. You still here?'

'I was just leaving. Carrot Top, come here . . .'

He edged tentatively a little closer, but was wary. Mouche said: 'I overheard everything. I couldn't help it. Aren't you ashamed?'

Carrot Top said: 'Oh,' and was lost in thought for a moment. Then the small boy with the red hair, bulbous nose, pointed ears and wistful, longing face, said reflectively: 'It was going to be quite queer without you. Oh yes, quite queer. At first I thought I might be able to go places again. You were always holding me down, you know . . .'

'Oh, Carrot Top – dear little Carrots,' Mouche said. 'I never wanted to.'

Carrot Top mused, 'I wonder. You were always pointing out my duty to Gigi, for instance. And there was never anything behind that pretty face. At first after you left, I thought I might be able to . . .'

'Yes, yes, I know – fly,' Mouche concluded for him, as the sudden tears filled her eyes and for a moment she was unable to see the booth or Carrot Top. 'Fly then, little Carrots. No one will keep you back now. Reach for the stars and they will tumble into your lap.'

The puppet emitted a mortal wail, 'But I don't want to fly, really. I don't want the stars. I only want to be with you for ever, Mouche. Take me with you.' He slithered across the counter and rested his head on Mouche's breast and beneath the pressure of the little figure she could feel the wild beating of her heart.

'Carrots – dear Carrots . . . I have always loved you.'

The doll turned his head and looked her full in the face. 'Do you? But you don't really love us, Mouche, not really, otherwise you couldn't go away.'

A moan of pain almost animal in its intensity was torn from Mouche. She cried, 'Oh, I do, I do. I love you all. I have loved you so much and with all my heart. It is only him I hate so terribly that there is room for nothing else, not even love any more.'

Standing there in the darkness, lost as it were in the centre of the vast universe of the empty stage, she could bring herself to speak the truth to a doll that she had never spoken to a human.

'I loved him. I loved him from the first moment I saw him. I loved him and would have denied him nothing. He took me and gave me only bitterness and evil in return for all I had for him, all the tenderness and love, all the gifts I had saved for him. My love turned to hate. And the more I hated him, the more I loved you all. Carrots . . . How long can such deep love and fearful hatred live side by side in one human being before the host goes mad? Carrots, Carrots . . . let me go . . .'

Yet she put up her hands and pressed the head of Carrot Top close to her neck and suddenly Mr Reynardo was there too, and the touch of the two little objects there made her wish to weep endlessly and hopelessly. She closed her eyes wondering if her mind would crack.

She was startled by the shrill voice of Carrot Top, 'But who are *we*, Mouche?'

The remark was echoed by Mr Reynardo, but when

she opened her eyes the pair were gone and instead, Monsieur Nicholas was regarding her from behind the panes of his square spectacles.

The little figure had the effect of calming her momentarily, for the old habits were still strong. Here was her reliable friend and philosopher and counsellor who appeared inevitably in the booth when matters threatened to get out of hand, mender of broken toys and broken hearts.

Yet he too asked the question that brought her again close to panic. 'Who are we all, my dear, Carrot Top and Mr Reynardo, Alifanfaron and Gigi, Dr Duclos and Madame Muscat, and even myself?'

Mouche began to tremble and held to the side of the booth lest she faint. Worlds were beginning to fall; defences behind which she had thought to live in safety and blindness were crumbling.

Who were they indeed? And what had been the magic that had kept them separate, the seven who were so different, yet united in love and kindness, and the one who was so monstrous?

Monsieur Nicholas spoke again. 'Think, Mouche. Whose hand was it you just took to you so lovingly when it was Carrot Top or Mr Reynardo or Alifanfaron, and held it close to your breast and bestowed the mercy of tears upon it?'

Mouche suppressed a cry of terror. 'The hand that struck me across the mouth . . .' she gasped and her own fingers went to her lips as though in memory of that pain . . .

'Yet you loved it, Mouche. And those hands loved and caressed you—'

Mouche felt her senses beginning to swim but now it was she who asked the question. 'But who are you then, Monsieur Nicholas? Who are you all?'

Monsieur Nicholas seemed to grow in stature, to fill the booth with his voice and presence as he replied: 'A man is many things, Mouche. He may wish like Carrot Top to be a poet and soar to the stars and yet be earthbound and overgrown, ugly and stupid like Alifanfaron. In him will be the seeds of jealousy, greed and the insatiable appetite for admiration and pleasure of chicken-brained arrogant Gigi. Part of him will be a pompous bore like Dr Duclos and another the counterpart of Madame Muscat, gossip, busybody, tattletale and sage. And where there is a philosopher there can also be the sly, double-dealing sanctimonious hypocrite, thief and self-forgiving scoundrel like Mr Reynardo.'

And Monsieur Nicholas continued: 'The nature of man is a never-ending mystery, Mouche. There we are, Mouche, seven of us you have grown to love. And each of us has given you what there was of his or her heart. I think I even heard the wicked Reynardo offer to lay down his life for you – or his skin. He was trying to convey to you a message from Him who animates us all . . .'

'No, no . . . No more!' Mouche pleaded. 'Stop. I cannot bear it . . .'

'Evil cannot live without good . . .' Monsieur Nicholas said in a voice that was suddenly unlike his own. 'All of us would rather die than go on without you . . .'

'Who is it? Who is speaking?' Mouche cried. And then on a powerful impulse, hardly knowing what she was doing, she reached across the booth to the curtain through which she could be seen but could not see and with one motion stripped away the veil that for so long had separated her from the wretched, unhappy man hiding there.

He sat there immovable as a statue, gaunt, hollow-eyed, bitter, hard, uncompromising, yet dying of love for her.

The man in black with the red hair in whose dead face only the eyes still lived was revealed with his right hand held high, his fingers inside the glove that was Monsieur Nicholas. In his left was crumpled in a convulsive grip the limp puppet of Monsieur Reynardo. It was as though he were the balancing scale between good and evil, and evil and good. Hatred and love, despair and hope played across his features, illuminating them at times like lightning playing behind storm clouds with an unearthly beauty, Satan before the fall.

And to Mouche who passed in that moment over the last threshold from child to womanhood, there came as a vision of blinding clarity an understanding of a man who had tried to be and live a life of evil, who to mock God and man had perpetrated a monstrous joke by creating his puppets like man, in His image and filling them with love and kindness.

And in the awful struggle within him that confronted her she read his punishment. He who loved only wickedness and corruption had been corrupted by the good in his own creations. The seven dolls of his real nature had become his master and he their victim. He could live only through them and behind the curtain of his booth.

And in one last blinding flash, Mouche knew the catalyst that could save him. It was herself. But he could not ask for her love. He would not and could not ask. In that flash she thought for an instant upon the story of Beauty and the Beast which had always touched her oddly as a child and knew that here was the living Beast, who must die of the struggle if she did not take pity on him.

Yet it was not pity but love that made Mouche reach her arms towards him across the counter of the puppet booth where they had duelled daily for the past year and cry: 'Michel – Michel! Come to me!'

No time seemed to have passed, yet he was out of the booth and they were clinging desperately to one another. Trembling, holding him, Mouche whispered: 'Michel . . . Michel. I love you. I do love you, no matter who or what you are. I cannot help myself. It is you I love, you that I have always loved.'

It was she who held him secure, his red head, as stiff and bristly as that of Mr Reynardo, sheltered in the hollow of her neck and shoulder where so often his hand, unrecognised, had leaned. And the desperation of his clinging was the greater as he murmured her name again and again: 'Mouche . . . Mouche . . . Mouche . . .' and hid his face from hers.

'Michel . . . I love you. I will never leave you.'

Then it was finally that Mouche felt the trickling of something warm over the hand that held the ugly, beautiful, evil, but now transfigured head, to her and knew that they were the tears of a man who never in his life had yielded to them before and who, emerging from the long nightmare, would be made forever whole by love.

And thus they remained on that darkened empty stage for a long while as Michel Peyrot, alias Capitaine Coq, surrendered his person and his soul to what had been so fiercely hateful and unbearable to him, the cloister of an innocent and loving woman and the receiving and cherishing of love.

Nor did they stir even when an old negro with a white patch over one eye shuffled across the echoing stage and looking down over the counter of the booth into the darkness of the mysterious quarters below chuckled.

'Oh ho; Little Boss! You, Carrot Top! Mr Reynardo!

Dr Duclos, Ali, Madame Muscat! Where are you all? You better come up here and learn the news. Miss Mouche is not going to leave us. She is going to stay with us for ever.'

LUDMILA
A legend of Liechtenstein

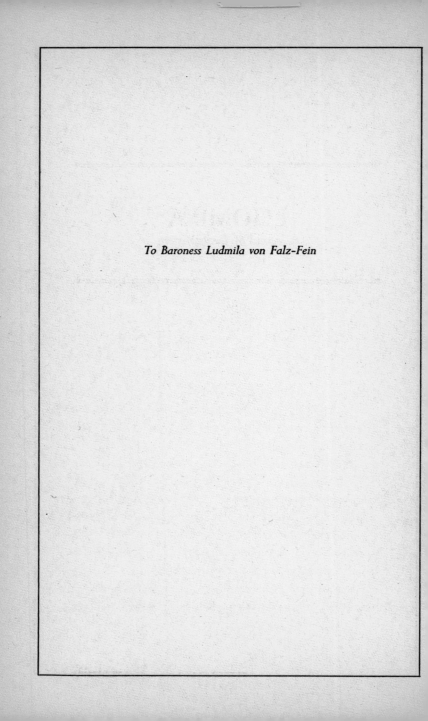

To Baroness Ludmila von Falz-Fein

PART WAY UP THE valley from Steg, in the Principality of Liechtenstein, where the torrent Malbun comes tumbling down its glacial bed from the peaks of the *Ochsenkopf* and *Silberhorn*, you will find the shrine of St Ludmila, *die heilige Notburga*, in a niche cut into the solid rock above the rushing waters.

It is a sweet figure in milkmaid's dress with the golden rays of the sun behind her head in place of the usual halo. In one hand she holds a harvesting sickle, and in the other a milk jug, for she is the patron saint of the dairymen, the herdsmen, milkers, butter separators and cheese-makers, and the taupe-coloured Alpine cattle with the broad heads, curving horns and large, gentle eyes are under her special protection.

Indeed, her connection with such is plain for all to see since beneath the feet of the figure there is affixed the whitened skull and greyish horns of what must once have been rather a small cow.

The younger generations, no longer brought up as were their fathers on the legends of the mountains, are unaware of its significance, but many of the local patriarchs remember what they learned at their mother's knee of the miracle that happened more than a hundred years ago, performed by the holy Notburga, the sainted milkmaid, the time of the annual return of the cattle at the end of the summer from the high pasturage to Vaduz in the Rhine Valley below.

All those connected with the event are long since dead: Alois, the bearded, hard-headed, chief herdsman and his brown-haired daughter, Ludmila, who was then only seven, and named after the saint, Father Polda, the mountain priest, chaplain of Steg, and of course the little Weakling, whose skull and horns adorn the shrine of the patron saint of all milch cows.

However, you may still see the gay and colourful ceremony that takes place in Liechtenstein each autumn when the first threat of snow comes to the high passes and the cattle begin to cough in the early gusts of cold wind that sweep down from the *Sareiserjoch* and the glaciers behind the *Wildberg* and *Panülerkopf*.

There is a valley tucked away behind the granite wall of the Three Sisters above Schaan, in Liechtenstein, the *Saminatal*, leading to Malbun, five thousand feet above the meandering Rhine. It is famous for its rich grass and quiet, protected pasturage, where are to be encountered from time to time scattered plants of that herb not found in the lowlands, one of the rare *Garbengewächse*, of the Species *Alchemilla*, which the Liechtensteiners call by the beautiful name of *Mutterkraut* — or 'Mother's weed', for it is believed to increase the flow of milk, and the herdsmen are invariably on the look-out for the yellow flowered broad-leafed plants which seem to grow best in those shaded spots where the snow has lain the longest during the winter when the valley is buried under snow and ice.

It is the custom of the peasants in Liechtenstein each spring to send their cattle up into the mountains and through the tunnel cut through a quarter mile of solid rock near Steg that gives access to this hidden, enchanted valley. They go in charge of herdsmen, dairymen and cheese-makers who move up with the beasts, taking their families with them in horse-drawn wooden carts.

There they remain for the entire summer, living in the high Alpine huts, tending the cattle at pasturage, milking them, making the rich yellow cheeses and creamy butter on the spot and keeping careful record of the yield of each animal. There is no contact with the valley below. Herds and herdsmen vanish not to reappear until mid-September.

But then, what a day!

The peasants come from miles around to gather at Gnalp, below the Kulm at the mouth of the tunnel. From Triesen, Vaduz Balzers and Schaan, in the *Rheintal* below, the citizens climb the mountain lining the winding roads, to cheer and wave to the returning wanderers, crowding as close as possible to see which and whose cow will be the first to emerge from the tunnel leading all the rest as signal of her championship.

The *Abfahrt* or descent takes place in the early morning with the sun shining over the *Rheintal*, warming the first nip in the clear mountain air. At first there is only the eager chatter of the citizens as they wait, the cries of children at play and the distant rush of mountain torrents. But then as a deep, hollow booming is heard from the dark recesses of the tunnel, an expectant hush falls upon the waiting throng. It is the sound of the giant bell of black metal cast especially for this occasion, and hung around the neck of the leading animal.

Louder and louder grows the clanging, as the herd approaches, stiller and stiller the people until with all the drama of a star actor suddenly bursting upon the stage, the champion of champions emerges into the light and stands for a moment, framed by the dark mouth of the tunnel.

She presents a strange and beautiful sight. Around her soft, fawn-coloured neck suspended from a shining dark leather collar hangs the huge copper bell decorated on all sides with silver hearts and stars and fitted with a silver clapper. This with her position as leader of the procession confirms her as best cow of the high pastures, best cow of the summer, best beast in the land.

On her forehead she wears a crimson heart or cross to

indicate her milk or cream has passed the average. But most striking of all, revealing her as first in her herd in yield of milk, butter and cheese, her one-legged milking stool has been affixed to the broad and noble head between the graceful sweep of the horns.

It is tied there upside down like the gay hat of a maid in spring, beribboned with streamers of the red and blue of Liechtenstein, crimson and white, silver and gold. A wreath fashioned of laurel leaves is woven about her head; cockades of red, white and blue are at her ears, bunches of meadow flowers make gay the leather of her collar.

One can only gaze at her with astonishment and admiration, for her simple, unobtrusive, natural beauty has been enhanced a hundredfold.

The procession winds out of the long tunnel and down the mountainside, the champions, the next best, the winners in minor classes, each with heart or cross, or milking stool bound upside down between their horns, then the horses garlanded and bedecked, drawing the family carts, the herdsmen and dairymen wearing rosettes of coloured ribbon on their shirts and crimson and azure cockades in their hats, bearing signs 'All of us are returning'. The signs too are cheered. No accidents, no illnesses, no deaths. God has been good. St Rochus and St Ludmila, the holy Notburga have watched over them and kept them from harm. Another year has passed. In the flower-garlanded carts the fat tubs of butter and the cheeses piled high like red and yellow cannon-balls denote prosperity and the wealth that the Creator, through nature, has seen fit to bestow upon his children.

And last of all, seemingly shamefaced, sad-eyed as though they knew that they had failed, without insignia, or touch of colour at horns or flank, unattended except for the work dogs yapping at their heels and the herdsman's apprentice bringing up the rear, come those animals of more common breed or less energy, who have failed to distinguish themselves in the production of milk, or the percentage of butter fat in their cream, or good solid proteins in the cannon-ball cheeses. From their unhappy expressions you would almost swear they knew they were inferior.

By the time they emerge from the tunnel there is no one left to greet them, or even notice them; the crowds had gone off down the mountain accompanying the colourful cavalcade of the successful beasts, leaving the others to bring up the rear as best they may.

It is a day of excitement, rejoicing and felicitation, with the owners of the winners crowding the cafés and opening bottles of red Vaduzer wine to the herdsmen and dairymen. It is a great occasion for the winners.

No longer in the general rejoicing and carousing incidental to this harvest ceremony is much thought directed towards the holy Notburga, that fourteenth-century milkmaid and simple serving girl who because of her piety, faith and devotion to the Virgin Mary, became a saint under her given name of Ludmila, devoted to the care of Alpine cattle and their herdsmen.

The skiers returning in the winter at dusk from the slopes of Malbun throw her hardly a glance, and the Ave that once used to be sung to her nightly by the herdsmen is now locked between the covers of a book instead of in the hearts of the people.

It was different in the old days before belief in miracles, magic and all the magical creatures that once inhabited the glens, ravines and dark forests, went from the mountains. Nature spoke more vividly to the people than it does today.

In those times there were still witches, elves, kobolds and little hairy wild men, good and evil fairies and saints that took on human guise and came down from Heaven to assist the pious or punish the wicked. Werewolves roamed the slopes and the scaly dragon with poisonous breath and deadly sting inhabited the rocky caverns. Even the great eagles perched on lofty crags, peering down in search of the whistling marmots, were regarded with superstition.

It was just at the end of this period and the beginning of modern times, so say the old men who remember this bit as told by their mothers, or that version handed down in an old mountain song, along with some yellowed sheets of notes left by Father Polda in the tiny chapel at Steg, that the strange affair of the little weakling cow who was deemed good for nothing took place.

Perhaps, it was not exactly as I am about to recount, for more than a century has gone by since these events happened, and the skull of the Weakling, as she was known, has weathered snow-white at the feet of St Ludmila where she stands benignly smiling in her niche. But the last time I visited her shrine I made my peace with her and asked in advance to be forgiven if I err. The expression carved on her countenance seemed to me tender and reassuring as though she knew that I too love these gentle and generous animals and have tried to do my best by one of them.

It was in the late summer of the year 1823; the herds were still pasturing in the Malbun and *Saminatals*, but the nights were already growing cool so that their days amidst the rich Alpine grass were numbered and the time of their annual descent into the *Rheintal* was not far off.

The setting sun had turned the blue sky a brilliant orange, then soft pink merging to pearl; the plum velvet of night had come out of the east, spangled with stars. The cattle were stamping and lowing softly in the stables nearby, the milking done and the herdsmen and dairymen gathered about the fire which the crisp air made welcome.

Father Polda had walked up, as was his nightly custom, from his little chapel in Steg, to sit and talk with the men and their families, for it was mostly under the sun and the stars that he preached, or sought the God that he served.

Alois, the Chief Herdsman, wrapping his cloak around him arose and awakened the echoes with the mournful cry of the ancient Ave he sent aloft each night:

'O-ho! O-ho! A-ve! Ave Maria!'

From the shadowed figures of the herders and dairymen around the fire arose the words and simple melody of the evensong of the herdsmen:

'God, the Father, Creator of Heaven and earth,
Give us your blessing, Watch o'er our hearth,
Dearly beloved Mary and your dearly beloved son,
Let your protecting mantle spread o'er every one,
St Peter, Thou watchman at Heaven's gate,
Shield us from savage beasts; in Thy hands our fate.'

The song swelled louder to include all the saints, Theodul, Rocchus, Wendelin and Veit, Sebastian and St Cyprian, each of whom had particular duties to protect them from the manifold dangers of the mountains, beasts of prey, witches, evil spirits, avalanches of rock and snow, the claws of the bear, the fangs of the wolf, the pounce of the lynx, the poisonous breath and the stinging tail of the dragon.

And of course there was Ludmila, *die heilige Notburga*, to whom they sang:

> 'Sainted Ludmila, milkmaid without blame,
> Make flow rich milk in Holy Maria's name,
> Fill every udder; speak thy word,
> To grace our beasts and bless our herd . . .'

Father Polda smiled in the darkness. None of the saints had been left out. A big, generous man, he was meticulous with regard to the catalogue of the holy, and even though those whose duty it was to deal with witches and dragons might be thought to have been outmoded by the modernity that was coming to the mountains, he was glad they were still included for politeness' sake and in memory of past favours, if nothing else.

Father Polda was a man of great and simple faith who believed in intercession, the force of prayer, and miracles, as opposed to Chief Herdsman Alois, who though professing belief, was hardheaded and as might be expected of one who lived out in the open and dealt with kine, practical and unsentimental.

Father Polda said: 'It has been a good summer – the holy Notburga has done her work well.'

Alois grunted in the dark and lit his long curved pipe until the sparks flew. 'There has been plenty of rain which has made the pasturage rich and the yield good,' he said. 'It will be better than last year.'

'Thanks be to God and St Ludmila who has interceded for us.'

Alois grunted again. 'St Ludmila has not been of much help to Johann Vospelt's weakling. Her yield is far below average. He was cheated when he bought that one.'

'Ah,' said Father Polda. 'The little one with the white muzzle and the ribs showing. It is a pity. Johann needs the money. He has not been well. He has a wife and small child. They spent all their savings to buy the cow.'

'She is hardly worth taking to pasture,' Alois declared. 'She costs more than she can repay. Vospelt would be better off to butcher and sell her. She could not even feed her calf properly. I put it to Schädler's Luzerner champion, who has enough over for a dozen such. There is a beast for you. Butter fat twelve per cent, second yield of cream after the first is skimmed and cheeses that weigh like stones.' He puffed at his pipe a moment and added: 'There is no animal in the herd that can touch her. She is practically certain to lead the procession for the second year for there is hardly more than a week left.'

Father Polda did not reply at once, but sat hugging his knees under the black cassock, a huge lump of a man crouched by the fireside looking up into the starry sky behind which were all his friends, and reflecting. Finally he said in a voice that was singularly soft and gentle to emerge from such a giant:

[183]

'How unhappy the little Weakling must be. How miserable and wretched. I shall say a prayer for her.'

Alois turned and stared at the priest over his pipe. 'An animal has no feelings. Pray that Johann Vospelt gets rid of her before she costs him more than she has already.'

But Father Polda was right, and Alois was wrong. The little Weakling was most miserable and unhappy indeed. For she was consumed by the hopeless desire to win the right to have her milking stool bedecked with gaily-coloured ribbons tied to her head at the summer's end.

It is doubtful whether she had dared dream of leading the procession down from the mountainside, wearing the laurel wreath and the big, copper bell, for such was far beyond the capacities of a small, not too well-bred cow.

But that spring, when with the others of the mixed herd owned by the poorer peasants, she had made her slow, toilsome way up the mountain, through the tunnel and into the high pasturage, she was sure that at the very least she could earn a crimson heart or cross for her owner, and what her simple, gentle soul yearned for most dearly was the decoration of the milking stool to wear upon her head.

But the sad truth, as she and the herdsman soon learned, was that she was not very strong and her capacity limited. She was small and thin, and on the whole not to be compared with the huge, sturdy Alpine breeds from whom the milk fairly poured in great, warm, frothy, fragrant streams. Her health was not of the best and there were days when she gave no milk at all.

She was not particularly handsome, lacking the broad head, wide-set eyes and long, curling eyelashes that gave the others the look of slightly ageing beauty queens. She was taupe-coloured, but darker and muddier in shade, thin flanked and high legged and differed further from the others by her white muzzle which made her look even paler and more delicate.

The Weakling tried very hard to be successful, but to little avail. As the weeks passed, she fell further and further behind in her yield. And the more she strained and fretted, the less she seemed to be able to produce.

She took her work seriously, eating heartily, cropping the long sweet grass indefatigably; she did not take too much exercise, or go climbing to higher pastures which might have disturbed her digestive processes; instead she lay quietly in the shade on hot afternoons, ruminating upon what it would be like to be crowned with the milking stool and cheered and acclaimed by the people. She chewed her cud carefully; she spent long hours thinking the proper thoughts about motherhood and the responsibility of producing milk.

But no matter how hard she tried she could not seem to succeed. When the milker came around to her and pegged his one-legged stool into the clay floor of the stable, he would say: 'Ach, it is hardly worth while to bring the pail to you, poor little Weakling.' Nevertheless he would milk her out of kindness, for he was a good man, but the result would be no more than a third of a pail, or perhaps even less as the season wore on, with no froth or body to it, but instead a thin bluish liquid that was deemed fit only to give to the pigs and chickens.

And the little Weakling would often turn her head and eye the slender, hand-turned milking stool, and so great was her yearning that she could almost feel what it would be like to have the seat touch her forehead between her small horns, and hear the rustle of the gaily-coloured ribbons as they bound it there. For hours afterwards, as she stood in her stall, the spot on her brow between the horns would ache with longing for the contact.

The reason that the Weakling so greatly desired the reward of the milking stool was that she was feminine and through no fault of her own had been denied the physique and constitution that would enable her to play the part for which she had been put on earth. She yearned to give lavishly the sweet milk that humans craved for their children and for themselves, she wished to see herself the creator of tubs of creamy butter and round cannon-balls of heavy yellow cheeses that would bring wealth to her owner. And female-like, she desired that adornment on the final day which turned the plainest of cows — which she had the misfortune to be — into the most ravishing creature. Capped with the milking stool, garlanded with paper flowers of all colours, beribboned in maroon and blue, she was sure she would please every eye and would arouse the admiration and appreciation of all.

You who believe that animals are dumb and incapable of reason or emotions similar to those experienced by humans will of course continue to do so. I ask you only to think of the yearning and heartache that is the lot of the poor and not-so-favoured woman, as she stares through the glass of the shop window at a gay Easter hat, a particularly fetching frock, the sheerest of stockings, or a pair of shoes with little bows that seem to dance all by themselves; lovable articles, desirable articles, magic articles out of her reach since she can neither buy them, nor earn them as a gift, yet things that she knows would transform her in a moment from someone drab and unnoticed, into a sparkling queen, a ravishing beauty that would draw all eyes to her. Or, if not all eyes, then at least a few, and if not a few, then just one pair of eyes, and in the end, the only pair that mattered.

How deep and melancholy is the wish to be beautiful and loved, to be lauded and admired, praised and desired. What power there lies behind the yearning within the feminine heart; what mountains have been moved, armies destroyed, thrones toppled, nations devastated, because of that feminine hunger for something bright, such as a ribbon, a bangle, a diamond, a crown, or the glitter in a man's eye. What civilisations have been built and worlds discovered to satisfy her craving for adornment, to confirm her belief that if only her body were outlined in silks from Cathay and her eyes ringed with kohl from Ind no man could resist her.

Can you really believe that such gigantic forces are engendered and shared only by humans, that this desire to be noticed and admired has not its counterpart in the animal kingdom?

If but the hundredth part of a woman's yearning from time to time for something beautiful to place upon her head, or at her throat, or in her ears, or on her back was what the little Weakling was experiencing in her desire to be distinguished as the most successful and desirable of her sex, then she was still the most miserable, unhappiest and most forlorn of all cows. For as the summer drew to a close she knew that her chances of succeeding were hopeless and that perhaps never in all her life would she taste that sweetness in the hour of triumph that was to come to her more fortunate companions.

It did not embitter her, however. It only made her sad, and increased the power of her yearning. She continued to see herself longingly, udders distended to aching with rich, creamy milk and hear the welcome sound as it frothed into the pail until it filled to overflowing. And then she would feel the milk stool upon her head.

But by the end of the summer, the little Weakling was

even more unprepossessing. She was gaunt, ungainly, her gait awkward, her udders slack and all but dry. Only her eyes preserved their luminosity and more than ever were filled with perpetual sadness.

One evening, when the herds had been grazing in the lower Samina valley and were returning to Malbun for the night, Father Polda came forth from his little chapel and joined leathery old Alois, the Chief Herdsman, for his evening walk, and side by side they marched up the path alongside the mountain torrent, conversing to the peaceful rushing of the water that mingled with the musical jangling and tonkling of the deep-toned bells around the necks of the cattle.

They discussed the forthcoming descent, the bounty of the year, the prices that would be fetched in the market by the season's yield of butter and cheese, which would mean prosperity for all the valley, all except poor farmer Vospelt whose weakling cow had yielded so little.

Thus the subject of the Weakling was revived, and Father Polda noted that they had already passed the shrine of St Ludmila in her niche in the rock. He had meant in passing to say another prayer for the little cow, to ask the holy Notburga to intercede not only for the unfortunate animal, but also for farmer Vospelt who needed the money so much for his family. He realised that it was too late for such intercession to do much good unless by a miracle, but he also believed there was no harm in trying.

They heard a sharp barking, and as they looked back they saw that Alois' work dog was yapping at the heels of the poor Weakling who as usual had fallen behind the others in the ascent, and was making no attempt to continue, nor was she paying the slightest attention to the animal baying at her heels.

Instead, as the two men gazed they could see that she had turned broadside to the path and was standing staring across the white-frothed torrent to the figure of St Ludmila, or rather the doll-like image of her that had been created by Anton the woodcarver of Steg, many, many years ago.

Since there were no pictures extant of *die heilige Notburga,* the woodcarver had taken the expression he had carved on her face from his own heart, one that had likewise loved the gentle members of the Creator's animal kingdom to whom He had assigned the task of extending the bounty of their motherhood to man.

Thus her smile was warm, tender, loving and yet infinitely pitying too and invited a similar expression to the lips of all those who passed and paused, and many, seeing her, would murmur: 'Dear St Ludmila, holy Notburga, give the sweetness and warmth of your protection to me likewise.'

And so the two men saw St Ludmila smiling down at the little Weakling, and the Weakling standing there, unmindful of the dog that other times would have terrified her, and gazing up at the holy Notburga, her eyes filled with hopeless and gentle pleading as well as the infinite longing and love that filled her being.

Alois said to Father Polda: 'Your little Weakling has grown impatient, waiting for your prayers.' He laughed good-humouredly. 'It looks as though she has decided to ask St Ludmila to intercede for her herself. She's gone one ahead of you, Father.'

But Father Polda was not amused, for the saints and prayer was something he took seriously, and he rebuked Alois angrily for levity verging on blasphemy.

'The Heavenly Father takes all animals both great and small under His shelter,' he said, 'but He did not give them the capacity to pray. That is for us to do for them, else He would have bestowed upon them the power of speech. You should not joke about such matters.'

Alois, who for all of his hard-headedness was a believer and who also was a little afraid of Father Polda, mumbled in his square brown beard that he had not meant to give offence, whistled to his dog and they turned up the mountain path again and soon the little Weakling came trotting after.

But this time it was perhaps Father Polda who was wrong, and the herdsman who could have been right.

For a prayer need not be a rhetorical address, or an itemised petition, or lips moved soundlessly inside a cathedral, or even words spoken into the air. A prayer may be a wordless inner longing, a sudden outpouring of love, a yearning within the soul to be for a moment united with the infinite and the good, a humbleness that needs no abasement or speech to express, a cry in the darkness for help when all seems lost, a song, a poem, a kind deed, a reaching for beauty, or the strong, quiet inner reaffirmation of faith.

A prayer in fact can be anything that is created of God that turns to God.

The little Weakling did not know that she was praying when she paused on the path, her eyes caught by the bright object shining from the niche in the rock. She was aware of nothing but the sadness in her being and an unutterable longing to pour forth her love in the shape of milk and thereafter to satisfy her yearning for the beribboned milking stool to be given her.

There is no way she could express or articulate this hunger, but it was particularly strong that evening as she returned with her udders almost flat. The figure in the rocks caught her gentle eyes. She turned to it in the moment when it seemed as though her unhappiness and shame would overwhelm her and she stood there trembling with the intensity of her desire to be as all the others and know the joy of giving as well as receiving.

And so, in a sense she made a prayer, and having done so, it existed; it was loosed. It was directed at the figure of the one whose love and duty called for her to intercede at the throne; and as with all prayers that arise from the sincere and loving heart, it was both heard and felt, in the far corners of the universe. For whereas evil has no power to extend beyond its own radius, the loving trust of a child, or the whispered confession of a sincere and tender heart can alter the stars in their courses. The gentle plea of a maid, asking for a bit of ribbon or cambric for her hair rings as loudly as the Cardinal's Latin in the outer spaces of time or thought, from whence destiny is directed.

Surely you do not think that God is angry at the desires of his creatures to win affection and appear beautiful and desirable in the eyes of the others. For He Himself loves beauty since He created so much of it on the face of the earth in both man and beast. And who but He caused the peasants of Liechtenstein to think of something so gay, innocent and charming as the wreathing of their beasts with laurel and garlands when the year's harvest was garnered, and crowning them with the insignia of their gentle servitude, the milking stool?

It was the next day, that Alois decided to take the cattle for the last time up to the highest pasture just below the *Sareiserjoch* where the green slopes are watered by crystal springs that gush from the rocks.

As the herdsmen and dogs marshalled the beasts for the climb, for the pasture lay a thousand feet above them, his eyes fell upon the Weakling, and he found himself torn between a mixture of annoyance as he remembered the reproof of Father Polda, administered the night before, and pity for the animal that was so thin and generally ill-favoured. He genuinely loved the animals that had been entrusted to his care, and watched over them.

As he looked, he thought of the long climb and the poor condition of the beast, as well as the plight of farmer Vospelt should the animal die on the heights and have to be sold for what her hide would bring for leather. And, too, there was the celebration and descent to be thought of, now less than a week away. It would be foolish to take chances, for it was a part of the custom that if during the season there was an accident, or one of the animals died, the ceremony of the milking stools, the ribbons and the gay decorations was dispensed with for that year.

He said to the herdsmen: 'Let her be, the little Weakling. She is not worth taking to the high pasture now. She is out of the running for the prizes, anyway. Let her remain down here where she will be safe.'

And then he called to his youngest daughter, aged seven, who was playing nearby, and who too was named Ludmila after *die heilige Notburga*: 'Ludmila, come here. Look after the little Weakling today and see that she comes to no harm. She is to remain behind. Do not let her stray out of your sight and see that she is back in the stall by sundown.'

And with that the dogs were set to work, the herdsmen cried 'Heuh!' Beasts and herders set off up the mountain.

Little Ludmila had brown legs and arms, a brown face, and brown hair, but her eyes were as blue as the cornflowers and wild delphinium that grew in the mountain meadows. She went at once and put her arms around the little Weakling's neck and laid her cheek next its soft, white muzzle, and then taking hold of the end of her halter marched off with her, with the Weakling following on docilely behind, her bell giving off a musical clang with every other step she took.

Some children would have been upset at having their day's play disturbed by such a peremptory order to take charge of a derelict animal that was not good for much of anything, but Ludmila was pleased, for she had for a long time wished to go into the dark glen at the foot of the *Bettlerjoch* a short distance away to look for elves which she was sure lived there.

She was afraid to go alone, for there might be other things there as well, such as witches, or little hairy wild men with peaked hats and long noses and ears who hid behind rocks with only the tips of their ears and the points of their hats showing, or even perhaps a small dragon.

But with the little cow along as her companion, her bronze bell tonkling loudly to frighten away any evil spirits, and her warm and comforting presence there and the halter to cling to, Ludmila felt no fear at all, and soon child and beast were lost to sight as they left the little community at Malbun and took the path towards

Gritsch and the deep wild glen at the bottom of the *Bettlerjoch*.

The sturdy brown legs took the child over a winding Alpine road that soon plunged into a dark pine forest. Shortly they came to a spot where the path split in two and on the right descended sharply into a dark and rocky ravine where fallen trees were tumbled like jackstraws and the boulders lay strewn about as though flung by a giant hand.

This was the mysterious ravine of the *Bettlerjoch*. Mounting, it grew wilder and more tumultuous until it reached to that mass of granite pillars and monoliths with the curiously human forms, which legend said were the Butter Beggars, those wandering friars who came over the pass known as the *Nenzinger Himmel* through the *Joch* to the high pasturage to beg for butter for the cold winter days to come and in return bestowed their blessings on herdsmen and herds and prayed for them, and who one day were overtaken by a terrible storm and their forms frozen there for ever.

But descending, the terrain grew less wild; there were little patches of grass and meadow with many herbs and wildflowers that seemed to flourish nowhere else.

For a moment, Ludmila hesitated to enter this unfamiliar territory, but the Weakling's bell jangled reassuringly, and when the animal also gave forth a soft 'Moo', she hesitated no longer, and taking the halter once more in her chubby fist entered the side of the ravine by the right-hand path and descended to the glen below.

The elves were there in the form of splinters of sunlight flashing from the quartz in the granite, or filtering through the greenery, dappling the leaves of the trees, and the child pursued them deeper and deeper into the ravine until they vanished in the darkness of tumbled rock or cave, or dense pines where the sun no longer penetrated.

Soon they came to a kind of glade opening out from the lower part of the glen through a rocky path. Here the land levelled for a space, a rushing brook quietened, as it meandered through this hidden meadow ringed with trees, and rich with sweet-smelling herbs and flowers, yellow blossoms with broad leaves amongst ferns, lichens and algaes, arenarias and saxifrages growing amidst dark grasses.

The little Weakling commenced to feed contentedly shaded by a gigantic oak tree that spread its branches in huge circumference and beneath which amidst a scattering of sweet acorns, the flowering herbs and weeds grew in thick profusion.

Comforted by the sound of the bell about the neck of the Weakling and her eager munching, Ludmila explored the boundaries of what was obviously a magic circle on enchanted ground; watching the long blue shadows of the trout as they sunned themselves in the brook, discovering a grey badger with shining eyes working at the mouth of his hole, startling a young deer, coming upon a whole family of little hamsters feeding on acorns and noting hundreds of tiny green-breasted finches and blue-headed tits flitting through the branches of the trees and peering out from behind the leaves.

And in this manner, with the Weakling feeding placidly, and the child, herself turned into the very kind of woodland and mountain elf she sought, playing in and about the beautiful glen and all its wild things, time passed. The shadows grew longer, the air cooler and the sun began to dip towards the jagged rim of the mountain peaks visible through the trunks of the tall pines, and her instincts told Ludmila that it was time to return home.

But the day had been long, exciting and strenuous, and she was both hungry and thirsty. And since she was a herdsman's daughter, Ludmila knew both where and how to provide herself with food and went directly to the source.

She secured the Weakling's trailing halter and led her to a sapling where she made her fast. Then seating herself at the hind quarters she took one of the soft teats, directed it at her mouth, closed her eyes, and began to milk.

At the touch of the little hands, so different from the rough, strong, horny palms of the herdsmen, it seemed as though a shudder ran through the Weakling. For the first moment as the child tugged, first at one then at

another, there was no response. Not even the thin bluish
trickle rewarded her efforts. But again, the shudder
shook the animal and she stood there, her feet spread
apart, trembling as though in the grip of a mountain
chill. All her pent-up anguish seemed to find expression
in the single cry, half a moo and half a moan, that came
from her throat and echoed from the pillars that
represented the frozen friars of the *Bettlerjoch* above and
went sighing off into the peaks. And then her milk began
to flow.

A few drops at first, then a trickle, then a stream, and
soon, a warm, rich, fragrant jet shot into the mouth of
Ludmila, causing her to gurgle and laugh with surprise,
pleasure and satisfaction, a sound which surely to the
Weakling must have been the most beautiful she had
ever heard. At last, she was giving, as God had intended
her to do.

The child drank until she could hold no more, and
thereafter led the Weakling to the stream to let her
refresh herself, and then taking her in tow, set off
through the rocky path that led from the enchanted
meadow, through the glen and up the ravine on the
homeward path. And for the first time since she had
matured, the Weakling, her heart filled with joy, felt the
ache of plenitude in her udders and the need to be
further relieved of the gift she carried there.

That night, when the herdsmen accompanying their
proud, sleek cattle returned from the high pasturage by

the *Sareiserjoch*, to the huts and stables just below the slopes of Malbun and the milkers took to their metal pails and one-legged milking stools, the miracle of St Ludmila, the holy milkmaid Notburga began.

The Weakling was already standing in her stall, emitting low moos, of pleasurable pain, when from force of habit the milker arrived at her side, set stool and pail, seized the nearest teat and squeezed perfunctorily, for he was weary from serving the heavy yielders and was grateful that the day was drawing to a close.

But the first sound of the powerful stream of milk landing with a clang at the bottom of the pail awoke him and caused him to cry out in amazement, as by the light of the lanthorn that hung from the roof of the milking shed he saw the distended skin of the swollen udders bearing such a burden as he had never encountered before in this unfortunate little animal.

He remembered the poor quality of her yield and still by habit, milked on, but when the pail was half-full, his cry arose over the stamping of the hoofs in the shed, the switching of tails and the rush of the milk — '*Hola*, Alois! *Hola* there, send for Alois! The Chief Herdsman is to come here at once to see what has happened.'

Alois came and stared likewise, for now the pail was three-quarters filled with creamy liquid topped by foaming bubbles of fatty froth, as rich as any that ever came from the big Swiss champions in the herd.

The pail was filled to overflowing, another was

placed beside her, once again the powerful jet of milk clanged against the empty sides, the liquid, warm and pungent, began to foam as it climbed up the pail. The other milkers and herders crowded into the shed as word spread of the astonishing thing that was happening to the little Weakling and a moment later there was a movement in the throng and the huge bulk of Father Polda bent over to pass through the door.

He glanced at the full milk pail, the second filling beneath the fingers of the milker, the colour of the fluid and the oily quality of the froth that topped it, and crossed himself.

'Holy St Ludmila, Holy Notburga!' he cried. 'It is a miracle!' for he wished it so.

Alois grunted as was his custom when he was about to become hard-headed and did not wish to admit something, especially to the priest. 'Some of these sickly ones come into milk late sometimes. We will see. The milk may be sour, or deficient. Wait until it has been separated.'

At last the udders were emptied, the second pail was nearly filled and taken away to be tested for fat and butter content, darkness fell, supper was eaten and the men gathered about the fire and once again the Mountain Ave rang out – 'O-ho! O-ho! A-ve! Ave Maria!' when the herdsman, whose duty it was to watch by night by the stables, came running into the circle, pale and out of breath:

'Alois! Father Polda! The one with the white muzzle, the little Weakling that was milked last tonight! I heard her complaining and went with the lanthorn to look. Her udders are filled again. She must be milked at once. Come and see if you do not believe me.'

It was true. Scarce three hours had passed, but the milk sacs were again distended and heavy with their burden. A milker was hastily summoned, and again the rich, yellowish liquid thundered into the pail; once more a second receptacle had to be fetched to hold the yield.

Father Polda crossed himself again and cried: 'Holy St Ludmila, a miracle, a miracle indeed. Well, Alois, what have you to say now?'

But the Chief Herdsman did not reply. He only stared bewildered at this amazing thing, though it was noted that he crossed himself likewise.

In the meantime, a layer of heavy, yellowish cream, six inches deep, and so thick that one might have stood up a spoon in it without its falling over, had gathered at the top of the first two pails that the little Weakling had filled earlier. Here was butter fat and a wealth of it such as had not been seen produced on the high pasturage within living memory.

All through the night and the next day and the next after that it went on. Replenishing herself, it seemed with no more than copious draughts from buckets of water, the Weakling continued to give of her so long withheld riches every three or four hours, wearing out relays of milkmen whose arms became heavy and fingers cramped as they worked to relieve her of her sudden wealth.

Word began to travel of the miracle that was taking place and mountaineers and woodcutters, keepers of hospices and charcoal burners from the neighbouring peaks and valleys came over to the milking shed in Malbun to see for themselves and soon there was no room inside for everyone and so the gentle little creature with the white muzzle, thin flanks and tender eyes was moved out into the open where all could see her and watch the fabulous torrents of milk that poured from her.

She stood there then in a kind of daze, wrapped in the glory of bestowing and the fulfilment of that part of her yearning that had to do with udders filled with life-giving food and drink that now was hers to share.

On the third day, the head dairyman came bustling from the cheese and butter factories next the milking shed in a state of excitement, shouting: 'One more pail, and the little one will win best of her group. She already has heart and cross won and needs only another gallon to catch up and surpass the best of her herd. It does not seem possible.'

It was Father Polda who replied: 'Oh, yes. With a miracle everything is possible, when there is faith in goodness and belief in the Creator whose will has called forth greater things even than this. She may even, who knows, be the first cow through the tunnel at Steg, bearing the bell and garland of victory — '

But here Alois and his hard head were heard from. 'That cannot be,' he said. 'Schädler's Luzerner has won the right of first cow by many tens of pounds. It will be impossible for the little one to overtake her. For the woodcutter who has just arrived over the *Bettlerjoch* tells me that the first snow has appeared on the *Panülerkopf* and the *Hornspitz*. Tomorrow we return to the valley.'

Father Polda sighed and said nothing, for the word of the Chief Herdsman in all things pertaining to the herds entrusted to his care was law, and no one dared question his commands. But it being Father Polda's first personal miracle, he wished to see it taken to the climax.

At that, the Weakling barely made the final pail that was needed to give her the honour of the milking stool. For the great and miraculous flow seemed at last to come to an end, and it was all that the milkers could do to wring the last drops from her fabulous udders. Yet achieve it she did though the effort left her weak and spent and she was led on tottery legs to the shelter of the stall, fed and watered and allowed to rest for the great event of the descent the following day.

And thus it was that the poor little Weakling whose hopes of realising her desire to be decorated with her milking stool, had seemed so utterly impossible of fulfilment, was led forth the next day, cleaned, washed, brushed, so that thin and emaciated as she was, her dun-coloured hide glistened. Hoofs and horns were polished until they sparkled in the sunlight and at last came the moment when she felt the seat of the milking stool pressed against her head between the horns by rough but kind hands and lashed there with gaily-coloured ribbons.

Streamers were fastened to the stool's leg, paper flowers and cockades attached to her headstall and about her ears; garlands of flowers hung about her neck. Small-boned, and lacking the stalwart maturity of the older animals, her head, graced by the decorations, her sweetness of expression gave her the air of a young girl going to her first ball. She became suddenly innocently beautiful and heart-warmingly radiant.

Now, word of the event that had taken place on the high pasturage had also reached to the village of Vaduz which heard the rumour of how the poor peasant Vospelt's animal that had been last in yield of dairy products had in the final three days, by the intervention of St Ludmila, poured forth a miraculous stream of milk.

Outside the tunnel, the crowds gathered to wait in twice the number they ever had before. They came up from Vaduz, the capital, and Schaan and Triesen, Mäls and Balzers, Nendeln and Eschen, to climb the lofty Triesenberg on foot and take up their position of vantage at Gnalp, to see for themselves whether there was any truth in the strange marvel that had been reported from the fastnesses of the high pasturage.

Because it might be an ecclesiastical affair, if true, the

Herr Canonicus Josef from the big church in Vaduz was there with lesser members of the clergy from the vicinity, and since if it were actually so it would redound to the eternal credit of Liechtenstein, a member of the ruling family from the *Schloss* below arrived, incognito of course.

Spontaneously, and without invitation, the brass band from Schaanwald appeared, the *Männerchor* from Planken and the girl singers from Mauren and Ruggell. The *Bürgermeister* of Vaduz came in his robes as did the president of the council and the ministers from Switzerland and Austria.

Naturally the attraction was likewise to see which would be the lead cow this year, but behind the huge turnout lay excitement of perhaps witnessing a marvel of some sort. It could of course hardly be true that the poor, sickly little animal they all remembered as belonging to peasant Vospelt, and which few had deemed worth even sending up to the high pasturage, could really have won a prize, much less the decoration of the milking stool, but if there was any truth in the rumours, they were all there and prepared to see.

In Malbun the cavalcade was ready for the descent. Cattle, horses, men, women, children, dogs, all were groomed and dressed in their best and decorated in every manner possible to mark the wonderful occasion.

An hour after sun-up the procession gathered on the meadow nearby the little community of huts, sheds and barns where they had all lived together during the long summer and the doors and windows of which were now boarded up.

Father Polda stood upon a drinking trough and blessed them, as was his custom, and sent up a prayer of gratitude to St Ludmila for the miracle she had created for them. Then with cries from the herders, the cracking of whips, the barking of dogs and the gay singing of the women and children, they started down the Malbun, next the roaring torrent to Steg.

First in the line, the silver clapper of the great brazen bell about her neck, booming her approach came Schädler's great champion Luzerner, winning beast the second year in succession, milking stool worn proudly as one who was used to such articles borne upon her head. Then came Gruber's Frisian, and Wohlmayr's Züricher champion in second and third place, followed by several others that had ranked high. Thereafter proudly heading the last division of the mixed herd belonging to many poor peasants tottered the little Weakling with her gay decorations and sweet exalted expression, looking like a mixture of half cocotte, half angel. At her head marched Ludmila, cornflowers the colour of her eyes braided in her brown hair. At her side walked Father Polda.

The three came eventually to the shrine of the holy Notburga by the torrent Malbun, and here they paused and turned to her as though by mutual understanding and consent, the huge man in the black cassock, the brown, barelegged child, and the Weakling. No word was spoken. Ludmila had her arm about the neck of the animal and together they stood by the wooden rail that guarded people from falling into the stream, and looked across the silvery waters to the figure in the niche, the sweet little doll with the tender expression on her carved and painted countenance.

On the child's face was wonder. In the eyes of the Weakling was deathless love. On the lips of Father Polda was a prayer. There they remained thus for a long time, so long that Chief Herdsman Alois returned to see what was holding up the procession and thus he found them.

When her father came up, the child suddenly left the little cow and ran to him, put her arms around his neck and began to cry, causing him to say: 'Now now, Ludmila, what is the matter? Why are you crying?'

'Because of my little cow who is so beautiful. St Ludmila wishes her to lead all the others.'

The Chief Herdsman was much less hard-headed when it came to his daughter and he smiled at her and said: 'She does, does she? And how would you know this?'

Ludmila stopped crying and took her father's hand and led him to the rail, looked across to St Ludmila and replied: 'Because she spoke to me, and *told me so*. Please, papa, let her be the first.'

Alois looked from his daughter to the Weakling, to Father Polda standing at her side and said harshly: 'What is this nonsense? Have you been putting ideas into the child's head? What does she mean the Saint spoke to her? Did you hear anything?'

Father Polda smiled, and gently shook his head. 'I heard nothing,' he said. 'But sometimes little children can hear things that we cannot.'

For a moment the big, bearded herdsman stood there staring at the statue. Then he picked up the child on his arm and strode away down the path. Man and beast followed.

But at Steg, the last stopping place before they moved down the *Saminatal* and entered the rock tunnel to emerge into the world beyond, Chief Herdsman Alois gave brief and sharp orders; two herdsmen came to the rear of the procession and led the little Weakling forward to the head of the line. There, while many looked aghast and all stared in utter amazement, they took the great black-silver star and heart-studded bell with the polished black leather collar from the leading cow and hung it about her neck. They likewise removed the crown of laurel leaves from the noble brow of the Luzerner champion and draped it about the head of the Weakling, for whom it was too big, and therefore fell slightly askew, giving her an even more coquettish air. In her emaciated state from the great effort she had made, the weight of the big bell was almost more than she could carry. Then the halter lead was put into the hands of Ludmila. The Weakling staggered forward and the two, now at the head of the procession, led the way down the road into the tunnel.

It was wrong, and arbitrary what Alois did, for Schädler's big Luzerner had fairly won the right to lead them all home a second year and one voice from the crowd protested, 'Halloo there, Mr Chief Herdsman, what is going on? Everyone knows that Schädler's animal is the winner.'

But with a terrible frown, Alois cried, 'Quiet! St Ludmila herself has commanded that the Weakling lead us home!' And thereafter none dared dispute his decision.

Soon the dense crowds lining both sides of the road on the other side of the tunnel heard the irregular booming of the big cowbell around the neck of the approaching leader. It would ring, then stop, then ring faintly, again louder as it approached, more faintly again, and once it jangled harshly as though the bearer had fallen.

Murmurs and shivers of excitement ran through the crowd. Louder and louder sounded the great bell and steadier now. The moment was at hand.

Out of the mouth of the tunnel stepped a brown elf with cornflowers the colour of her eyes braided through her brown hair, leading a small thin cow with a white muzzle, belled, crowned and garlanded. For a moment they stood blinking in the sunlight. Then a great shout went up from the throng, almost like a hosannah, a cheer and a cry and a greeting and a prayer all in one. Men waved their hats and shouted, women wept and sobbed.

It was true. The miracle had taken place, for there was the evidence before their very eyes. Not only had the poor despised Weakling won the right to wear her milk stool, but the champion's laurels and winner's position, the prize of best cow of the year had come to her. Only a saint could have made this possible.

Then the brass band struck up the national anthem of Liechtenstein, the *Männerchor* burst into song as did the *Sängerbund* of girls from Mauren and Ruggell, and the women's choir from Triesenberg.

His Highness, the member of the Royal Family, dropped his incognito and stepped forward to pin a glittering medal, the Royal Double Eagle First Class, to the Weakling's collar and pick up the child Ludmila in his arms and kiss her. Herr Canonicus Josef suddenly knelt in the road, followed by the other members of the clergy, and struck up an 'Alleluia' and the next moment men, women and children in the huge throng of welcomers likewise went to their knees, singing and giving thanks to Him and those on High from whom all miracles and blessings flow.

And so, her greatest desire and dream of glory come to realisation, the little Weakling, burdened with the earthly prizes awarded to her by Heavenly dispensation, looked out upon this strange scene, the towering mountains opposite, the blue thread of the Rhine in the valley far below, the people in their Sunday best kneeling in the road, the black-robed priests, the stately figure of His Highness, and her eyes were gentle and swimming, filled with love and happiness, that all this which she had so much desired had in the end happened to her, and that before her final moment she had been privileged to give.

For the effort and the strain of the last three days had been too much for her, and with that sure instinct of animals, she knew she was looking upon the sunshine and the kindly people whom it had been her duty to feed for the last time. And she was content.

The big bell boomed again. The sun glittered from the golden medal at her collar. Child and animal started forward again down the mountain followed by the gay and colourful procession of the annual return from the high pasturage.

There is not much more to the story. Worn out by her efforts, the little Weakling passed away in the valley before sundown that evening. Yet strangely it did not put a damper on the celebration, or the happiness of the people at having been singled out for the execution of a miracle in their midst. They and the Canonicus saw it quite simply as the logical extension of the miracle whereby having performed it and demonstrated her love and power via the Weakling, St Ludmila, the holy

Notburga, had taken the little animal to her as her reward and she would henceforth graze peacefully and happily in the Heavenly pastures close to the side of her loving friend and patron. And it is for this reason that the skull and horns of the Weakling were bestowed on the shrine of the Saint.

The butter and cheese made from the miraculous milk of the Weakling brought their weight in gold and never again would the poor peasant Vospelt or his family want for anything.

Only one thing more remains to be told.

A week later, Chief Herdsman Alois suddenly appeared at Steg in the Samina valley with the child Ludmila at his side and sought out Father Polda in the tiny chapel.

'Come,' he said to the priest. 'Come with us.'

They walked, all three in silence, up the path again past the shrine in the rocks to which Alois did not so much as vouchsafe a glance now, until they came to the deserted huts and barns on the Malbun slope. Here it was that the little Ludmila at her father's behest took over the leadership, and with the sure orientation of the mountain child, led them up the path to the *Bettlerjoch*. As she had once before, she branched off from the main dark and fearsome ravine downwards towards the glen of the elves, and thence through the rock path to the magic circle in the enchanted meadow peaceful in the morning sun with only the sound of birds in the great oak, the rustling of small animals in the underbrush and the gentle murmur of the stream resting before it resumed its plunge below.

Alois now roved about this meadow, his eyes on the ground; he went to the brook, came back, knelt near the oak tree and examined the ground, arose and went to the opposite side and did the same. And as he searched, his dark, bearded face lit up with satisfaction and at last he came over and faced Father Polda.

'Well,' asked the priest. 'Why have you brought me here? What is it you have discovered?'

'This,' said Alois. 'Look there. Do you recognise that little weed with the yellow flowers and the broad leaf?'

Father Polda gazed down at the plant that seemed to be growing in unusual profusion all about them. 'It is the *Alchemilla*,' he replied. 'The *Mutterkraut*.'

'Yes,' said the herdsman. 'Have you ever seen so much at one time?'

The priest shook his head. 'No. It is most unusual.'

'Ah! Then come here and look. Here under the oak tree, it grows almost solid. But see where it has been cropped, and the hoof-marks of an animal. Round and about this tree it has been eaten away — '

'Well — ?' said the priest.

Alois threw him a look of triumph. 'It was here that Ludmila came that day with the little Weakling when I refused to take her along to the high pasture. Those are her hoof-marks. The little one in a few hours found and consumed more *Mutterkraut* than most Alpine cattle would in a lifetime. The whole day she grazed upon the *Alchemilla*. In the evening her milk glands violently stimulated, she started to give milk.' He smiled in triumph again and looked the priest in the eye. 'There is your miracle of St Ludmila for you. It is explained as I always knew it must be.'

The priest remained silent and his eyes were bent to the ground where the hoof-prints of the little Weakling were still plain to be seen as well as the close-to-the-ground cropped ends of many of the *Alchemilla* plants which somehow had flourished in this secluded place.

'Well,' asked the Chief Herdsman, 'what have you to say?'

The priest looked up, but his brow was unclouded and his eyes untroubled and clear. 'Yes,' he said finally. 'You are right. The miracle is indeed explained for all of those for whom the miracles must always be explained lest they be forced to confess that they are not as important as they believe themselves to be.'

Alois said: 'You admit then that now we know why all of a sudden the Weakling gave so much milk and of such high content that in the end it was like giving her heart's blood and strength and it killed her?'

A little smile now played about the lips of the big priest. 'That is correct,' he said. 'Now we know why the little one suddenly gave so much milk. Ah, yes, now we know everything.'

'Eh?' said Alois, suspiciously, struck by something in the tone of the priest. 'What do you mean by everything?'

'Oh,' replied Father Polda, still smiling, 'all the other miracles which you will explain to me – what made you say that day the little Weakling was praying at the shrine of St Ludmila, what was it that led you to decide against taking the animal to the high pasturage that day, how you came to entrust her to little Ludmila's care – also of course how the child came to wander here to this deserted glen where no ordinary child would venture alone, and how together they discovered this marvellous patch of *Mutterkraut* – and finally of course the greatest wonder of all, what made you decide in one moment to listen to your child, go against the records and at the last minute name the Weakling champion cow and leader of the descent into the valley, thus setting the final stamp and seal on the miracle in which you do not believe?'

He paused and offered his hand to the child who took it confidingly. 'Come,' he said, 'let us go from here.' He turned to Alois still smiling gently, 'But there will be time for those explanations later — '

He walked slowly hand in hand with Ludmila back the way they had come through the rocky defile. Behind them Alois walked silently, his head bent towards the ground as one in deep thought . . .

FOR THE BEST IN PAPERBACKS, LOOK FOR THE

In every corner of the world, on every subject under the sun, Penguin represents quality and variety – the very best in publishing today.

For complete information about books available from Penguin – including Puffins, Penguin Classics and Arkana – and how to order them, write to us at the appropriate address below. Please note that for copyright reasons the selection of books varies from country to country.

In the United Kingdom: Please write to *Dept E.P., Penguin Books Ltd, Harmondsworth, Middlesex, UB7 0DA.*

If you have any difficulty in obtaining a title, please send your order with the correct money, plus ten per cent for postage and packaging, to *PO Box No 11, West Drayton, Middlesex*

In the United States: Please write to *Dept BA, Penguin, 299 Murray Hill Parkway, East Rutherford, New Jersey 07073*

In Canada: Please write to *Penguin Books Canada Ltd, 2801 John Street, Markham, Ontario L3R 1B4*

In Australia: Please write to the *Marketing Department, Penguin Books Australia Ltd, P.O. Box 257, Ringwood, Victoria 3134*

In New Zealand: Please write to the *Marketing Department, Penguin Books (NZ) Ltd, Private Bag, Takapuna, Auckland 9*

In India: Please write to *Penguin Overseas Ltd, 706 Eros Apartments, 56 Nehru Place, New Delhi, 110019*

In the Netherlands: Please write to *Penguin Books Netherlands B.V., Postbus 195, NL–1380AD Weesp*

In West Germany: Please write to *Penguin Books Ltd, Friedrichstrasse 10–12, D–6000 Frankfurt/Main 1*

In Spain: Please write to *Longman Penguin España, Calle San Nicolas 15, E–28013 Madrid*

In Italy: Please write to *Penguin Italia s.r.l., Via Como 4, I-20096 Pioltello (Milano)*

In France: Please write to *Penguin Books Ltd, 39 Rue de Montmorency, F-75003 Paris*

In Japan: Please write to *Longman Penguin Japan Co Ltd, Yamaguchi Building, 2–12–9 Kanda Jimbocho, Chiyoda-Ku, Tokyo 101*

BY THE SAME AUTHOR

'It is almost impossible not to succumb to Mr Gallico's spell' – *The Times Literary Supplement*

Jennie

Original, humorous, poignant, compassionate, *Jennie* has become a classic of its kind: the unforgettable adventures of a small boy changed into a stray cat and befriended by the indomitable Jennie, who initiates him into the lore of London's streets.

'*Jennie* has the same simplicity as *The Snow Goose*; it is, like its forerunner, a family book, and as such deserves the same success' – *The Times Literary Supplement*

Thomasina

'I was always aware, from the very beginning, that I was a most unusual cat . . .'

Thomasina, beloved ginger cat of Mary Ruadh, has a strange story to tell – that of her own murder at the hands of Mary's father, a hardworking country vet who breaks the heart of his daughter when he destroys her injured pet.

Rescued by the gentle Red Witch of the glen, Thomasina becomes Talitha, feline descendant of an Egyptian cat-goddess . . . and sets out to wreak dreadful revenge on her slayer.

Mrs Harris Goes to New York

''Old on to your hair, Vi, I've got something to tell you. We're going to America!'

With this startling remark, another glorious adventure begins for the indomitable London 'daily' Mrs Ada Harris (pronounced 'Arris) and her timid friend Mrs Butterfield.

'There seems to be no limit to Mr Gallico's ability to produce small miracles' – *The Times*